Everyone's talking about Frankie!

"As soon as I opened *Fizzy Pop* I knew this was going to be a fantastic read! From the very first word Frankie spoke, I realised she was going to be my friend."
Imogen, age 12

"Original, funny and well-written, you just can't put *Fizzy Pop* down. I loved getting to know the characters through the story, especially Frankie, and her here-to-help attitude was really hilarious. The book was a real page-turner; I read it in one night it was that captivating."
Beth, age 9

"This book is addictive! It's funny and brilliant with great characters and a fantastic storyline. Frankie Foster's adventures are gripping with lots of twists – I could not put it down!"
Zoe, age 12

Also by Jean Ure

FRANKIE FOSTER

Fizzy POP!

Here to Help!

Jean Ure

HarperCollins *Children's Books*

First published in Great Britain by HarperCollins *Children's Books* 2011
HarperCollins *Children's Books* is a division of HarperCollins*Publishers* Ltd,
77-85 Fulham Palace Road, Hammersmith, London W6 8JB

The HarperCollins *Children's Books* website address is
www.harpercollins.co.uk

1

FRANKIE FOSTER : *Fizzy Pop*
Text copyright © Jean Ure 2010

ISBN-13 978-0-00-736265-3

Printed and bound in England by
Clays Ltd, St Ives plc

Mixed Sources
Product group from well-managed
forests and other controlled sources
www.fsc.org Cert no. SW-COC-001806
© 1996 Forest Stewardship Council
FSC

FSC is a non-profit international organisation established to promote the
responsible management of the world's forests. Products carrying the FSC
label are independently certified to assure consumers that they come
from forests that are managed to meet the social, economic and
ecological needs of present and future generations.

Find out more about HarperCollins and the environment at
www.harpercollins.co.uk/green

For my editor, Rachel Denwood,

who sowed the seeds.

Everyone seemed to think it was my fault that Rags ate the rissoles. I always get the blame for everything! Like when I encouraged one of my best friends to try and trace her birth mother. Mum said I shouldn't have interfered. But I wasn't interfering! I just wanted to help.

CHAPTER ONE

"FRANKIE FOSTER!" My sister's voice came shrilling down the stairs. *"Was this you?"*

Uh-oh. Trouble!

Guardedly, I said, "Depends what you're talking about."

"This. This is what I'm talking about!"

She stood, quivering with rage, on the top step, waving a bit of rag. Well, at first glance it looked like a bit of rag. At second glance I could see that it was in fact her pink-and-white stripy shirt that I had kindly ironed for her just the other day. Unfortunately, there had been a slight problem with the iron; it had got too hot, or something. Obviously faulty. I find that a lot of the things I have to deal with turn out to be faulty. It is somewhat discouraging.

"*Well?*" Angel thumped impatiently on the banister rail.

I said, "Well—"

"I know it was you, so don't bother trying to deny it!"

I hadn't been going to deny it. I suppose I have my failings, same as anyone else, but I do try to be truthful whenever I can.

"There's something wrong with the iron," I said.

"There's nothing wrong with the iron, you *idiot*!"

"There must be," I said. "It didn't do that to the other things. It was only when I got to your shirt it went funny."

"Oh, for God's sake!" She was shrieking now. She does a lot of shrieking. "Eleven years old and you haven't even learnt how to use an iron properly!"

I resented that, considering I'd done a whole load of sheets and pillowcases without so much as a single wrinkle. I was proud of my ironing!

"Maybe," I said, "it's something to do with your shirt."

"Yes, you're supposed to use the iron on cool, you moron!"

I said, "Oh." And then, "How was I to know?"

"It says it right here, on the label, if you'd just bothered to look!"

"You don't have to yell," I said.

"I do have to yell! Yelling's the only thing that keeps me sane. It's the only thing that stops me putting my hands round your throat and throttling you! It's—" She stopped.

"What are *you* pushing for?"

"Excuse me," said Tom. "I'm just trying to get down the stairs."

"There's no need to *push*. As for you, Frankie F—"

"What's going on up there?" Mum had come out of the kitchen, accompanied by Rags. Rags is our dog; he loves a bit of excitement. "What's all the shouting about?"

"It's them," said Tom. "They're at it again."

"I'm not at it," I said. "She's the one making the noise."

"You're lucky that's all I'm doing!"

"Oh, for heaven's sake," said Mum. "What's the problem?"

"She is!" shrieked Angel. "Look what she's done!"

She hurled her shirt viciously down the stairs in a scrunched-up heap. What dog could resist? Rags was on it in an instant. Angel let out one of her ear-splitting screeches.

"Stop him!"

I made a grab, but Rags was too quick. He capered off joyously down the hall, shaking the shirt from side to side like it was a rat. Angel screeched again. Dad says when she does that it is like a car alarm going off inside your head.

"Rags!" Mum cornered him at the end of the hall. "*Drop!* Bad boy!"

He wasn't a bad boy, he just thought it was a game. Any dog would have thought it was a game. But he always obeys Mum, I don't know why. He doesn't take any notice when I tell him to do things. I think it's because we're mates, while Mum is an authority figure. She can be really stern when she wants. Which, now I come to think of it, is quite often.

"Right. Now!" Mum held up the shirt. "What's the matter with it?"

"She's gone and shrivelled it," wailed Angel.

"Only a little bit," I said. "If you tucked it in,

nobody'd ever notice."

"I don't want to tuck it in! That was my favourite shirt, I was going to wear it on Saturday. Mum, it's not fair! She shouldn't be allowed to touch my things."

"Frankie." Mum turned to look at me. She didn't seem cross; just kind of… resigned. "I told you to stick to simple stuff… sheets, pillowcases. Tea towels. Why did you have to go and mess with Angel's shirt?"

"It was there," I said, "waiting to be ironed. I thought you'd be happy! I folded everything all nice and neat. *And* I put it all away."

"*And* you went spying in my room!"

"Did not!"

"Did so!"

"Did *not*. I just put it away for you."

"Just tried to hide it, you mean."

I hadn't actually tried to *hide* it, cos that would have been dishonest; but I had sort of hoped that by the time she came across it she'd have decided it was just, like, totally naff and she couldn't bear to be seen dead in it, which is what usually happens when she's worn something more than a couple of times.

"You might at least have owned up," said Mum. "Just admitted to an honest mistake."

"Honest!" Angel made a loud barking sound. "Huh!"

Whatever that was supposed to mean.

"Look, just calm down," said Mum. "It's not the end of the world. We'll get you another one."

"*She* ought to buy it."

"Well, I can't," I said, "cos I haven't any money."

"No, that's because you're still paying for setting the garden shed on fire!"

"That was an accident."

"Are you saying my shirt wasn't?"

"No, I—"

"Are you saying you shrivelled it *on purpose*?"

"No! I just—"

"STOP!" Mum's voice came bellowing at us up the hall. "I have had enough!"

We both quavered into silence. When Mum gets mad, she gets really mad. Far worse than Dad.

"Just button it! I can't take any more, this time of the morning. I've got Mrs Simmonds coming for a fitting at eight o'clock, I don't need to be all hot and bothered."

Mum works from home doing dressmaking and stuff; she often has people arriving at weird hours.

"Get yourselves ready," she said, "and get off to school."

Angel disappeared, muttering, into her room. I went through to the kitchen to eat some breakfast. I always eat breakfast. I once read somewhere it's the most important meal of the day; it gives you brain power. Angel doesn't bother with it, on account of being figure-conscious. The most she ever has is a low-fat yoghurt, but I believe in eating properly. Angel can be stick thin if she wants. I'd rather *not* have my stomach rumbling in front of the whole class, which is what happened to me once and was just, like, so embarrassing I wanted to die, especially when people started calling me Rumblebelly. Who wants to be stick thin anyway? She is at that age, Mum says. Fifteen. It makes her very angry.

Tom was in the kitchen, packing books into his school bag. I said, "You eaten?" but he just mumbled and went on packing. I have never actually seen Tom eat breakfast, but that's not to say he doesn't. He is just a very private kind of person. Very *secretive.* I have this theory that Mum must have been abducted by aliens and that his real father is some kind of robot creature from outer space. It seems the only rational explanation. Mum says I'm not being fair; she says he is just shy. "Imagine what it must be like for him, sandwiched between you two."

At least he doesn't fly into rages.

"Honestly," I said, "talk about over the top! It was just a little bit of crinkle."

I'd hoped he might sympathise with me for the way I'd been treated; that we might even have a cosy chat about Angel and her furious temper. But you can't really have cosy chats with Tom.

"It's not like I crinkled the whole thing," I said. "Soon as I saw what was happening, I stopped."

Tom grunted, and stuffed some more books into his bag.

"And that thing with the shed… I was just trying to fumigate it."

"Yeah?"

"For Dad."

"Yeah."

"Cos of what he was saying about someone leaving the door open and the foxes getting in?"

"Yeah?"

"Saying it smelt bad, it needed to be fumigated?"

"Yeah?"

"I thought I'd do it for him."

Tom wedged in the last of his books. "Surprised you knew what fumigate meant."

"I Googled it!" I'm not stupid. I know how to find things out. "It's when you fill a place with fumes to get rid of smells and stuff."

Which is what I'd done. *Tried* to do. I'd taken one of the big scented candles left over from Christmas and put it on Dad's work bench and lit it. I'd stood it on a saucer! I'm not irresponsible.

"I was only trying to help," I said.

"Some help," said Tom.

I'd thought Dad would be pleased. I thought

next time he went out there he'd find a lovely scent of pine. Instead, there'd been a horrible smell of burning. Mum had been a bit cross. She said who on earth would leave a lighted candle in a shed full of combustible materials, meaning stuff that would go up in flames. Angel said, "*She* would!"

I felt a bit bad about it cos I had this feeling it might have been me that had left the shed door open in the first place. It might not have been; but it could have been. Which is why I very nobly offered to give up two weeks' pocket money to help pay for the repairs. I never thought Dad would accept!

"I still don't know how it happened," I said.

"Yeah." Tom picked up his bag and slung it over his shoulder. "A total mystery."

"Well, it is!" I agreed, eagerly. It *was* a mystery. It's what I'd been saying all along, only no one would listen. "Might not have been my fault at all," I said. "Someone might have gone in there and knocked the candle over. A burglar, or something. Don't you think?"

But Tom had gone. He is a most unsatisfactory person to talk to. I slathered some marmalade over a piece of toast and wandered up the hall in search of Mum. She was in the front room, preparing stuff for Mrs Simmonds.

I said, "Mum?"

"What? Why haven't you left for school? Frankie, *please* don't let that dog in here! I've asked you before… not when I have someone coming."

"OK." I squashed Rags back out and closed the door.

"And don't eat over Mrs Simmonds's clothes!"

"I'm not." I moved away. "Mum, about Angel's shirt… *I* didn't know it would shrivel! I was only trying to help."

Mum sighed. "Yes, I'm sure you were."

"You have so much work to do!"

"I do," said Mum, "don't I? And you're just making even more for me, standing there dropping toast crumbs on the floor."

"Sorry," I said, "sorry! I'll get the vacuum cleaner."

"No! For God's sake! I mean… it's all right," said Mum. "I'll see to it. You just get yourself off to school."

"All right." I crammed in my last bit of toast. "Abow a garn sh—"

"I beg your pardon?" said Mum.

I swallowed. "About the garden shed… you don't think a burglar got in there, do you?"

"Not really," said Mum. "No."

"It could have been a burglar! He could have knocked the candle over. He could have done it *deliberately*."

"Oh, Frankie," said Mum, "just go to school!"

"I was only asking," I said.

Burglars did that sort of thing. Seemed far

more likely to me than a big fat candle falling over all by itself.

"Frankie, will you *please*—"

"Yes, yes, I'm going!" I said.

I reached the front door at exactly the same moment as Angel.

"I hope you don't think you're going to walk with me," she said.

I used to have to walk with her when I was in primary school; either with her or with Tom. Angel used to complain that Tom was always wriggling out of it.

"Just because he's a boy!"

She doesn't like being seen with me in public, she says I'm an embarrassment and that I cramp her style, whatever that is. I can't say I particularly like being seen with her; not when she's always flying into rages. It's like being out with a crazy person. I tossed my head and told her that she didn't need to worry.

"I'm meeting my friends."

"Friends?" Angel snorted. "I'm surprised you've got any! Wait till you start shrivelling *their* favourite shirts."

We sidestepped elaborately as we went through the door. I took a pace backwards.

"Age before beauty," I said. I thought that was pretty good. I'd been dying to use it ever since reading it in a book.

Angel stuck her face close to mine.

"You are a hideous child," she said. "I find you unspeakably loathsome."

She is totally mad. I feel sorry for her.

CHAPTER
TWO

Angel went stalking off, wobbling slightly in her designer shoes. Sling backs, with long pointy toes and tiny little spike heels. She has to take them off once she reaches school and put on her ordinary flat black ones, same as the rest of us. *Clodhoppers*, she calls them. I don't personally mind clodhoppers. The way I see it, if a herd of maddened elephants suddenly came roaring down the street you would at least be able to make a run for it.

Angel wouldn't; she would be crushed underfoot. It's pathetic, really. Risking life and limb just to impress boys. Cos that's all it is. It's all about boys. She does have good legs, though.

I watched her receding into the distance. I suppose in her way she has style. I could see that as a stolid ten-year old, dumping along at her side, I probably had cramped it for her. I am not really what you would call a fashion accessory.

I humped my bag over my shoulder and stomped on. I know that I stomp cos Miss Henderson, our PE teacher, has told me so. She said, "My goodness, Frankie! You're a bit of a stomper." It is just the way I am built. Mum says I am "four square and solid". Angel, on the other hand, cos of only eating low-fat yoghurt, is all frail and wispy. She'd be an easy target for elephants. I reckon a flock of sparrows could crush her.

Skye was waiting for me on the corner of Barlow Road. We meet up there every morning; me, and Skye, and Jem. Skye Samuels and Jemma McClusky are my two best mates. We were all at primary school together, and we all live near each other.

I said, "Hi."

Skye said, "Your sister's just gone marching past with her nose in the air. I said hello but she, like, totally ignored me?"

"She's in one of her rages," I said. "Just cos I shrivelled her shirt."

"You shrivelled her *shirt*?"

"Only a little bit! You wouldn't hardly notice. But you know what she's like."

"I know what *you're* like," said Skye.

What was that supposed to mean? I decided to pretend she hadn't said it.

"It was kind of surreal," I said. "She just totally lost it. Got all frothed up and went into this furious megasulk, yelling and carrying on, saying it was her favourite shirt and I'd gone and ruined it."

"People are so unreasonable," said Skye.

Well, I do think they are, and especially my sister. *Angel*. Her name is actually Angeli, but everyone calls her Angel, which if you ask me is a big laugh considering she is anything but. For one thing she is totally vain, always gazing at herself in the mirror and thinking how beautiful she is. For another, there's this humungous temper that she has. Mum says she will grow out of it, it is just a teenage thing, but I personally reckon she should be sent to anger management classes.

"No sane person," I said, "would get all worked up over a tiny bit of shrivel. It was only on the edge." I hoicked up the edge of my shirt to demonstrate. "*There*. Just *there*! It's not normal."

"Seems to me," said Skye, "shrivelling the edge of someone's shirt isn't exactly what you'd call normal."

"I didn't do it on purpose! I was *ironing*," I said. "I was trying to *help*. The thing just went and shrivelled before I could stop it."

"You mean you had the iron too hot."

"I didn't have it too hot, it got too hot." Why did everyone keep trying to put the blame on me all the time? "I reckon it must have been getting too much electricity or something. It's what happens, it all comes rushing through the mains." I know about things like that; Dad's an electrician. "Power surges," I said. "I bet that's what it was."

"So why didn't you just turn it down?"

"Cos I didn't know! You don't, with power surges. They just happen. Suddenly. Anyway," I said, "I'm sick of talking about it. Where's Jem?"

"Dunno."

"She's late!"

Skye looked at her watch. "If she doesn't arrive soon we'll have to go or we'll miss registration and that'll be our names in the Book."

"Ooh!" I shivered. "Don't want our names in the Book!"

"It's not funny," said Skye. "You can get into a whole load of trouble."

"Only if you're in it three times."

"I don't want to be in it *one* time, thank you!"

Skye is a very law-abiding sort of person, it really upsets her if she breaks a rule, like by mistake or not knowing about it. According to her, rules are there to be obeyed. Mostly, on the whole, I do obey them, cos it's no fun being told off, but I sincerely believe that you have to exercise your own judgement and not just blindly follow. Like at our school, Hillcrest, we have this rule about not eating in the street. What kind of a rule is that? You could be dying of starvation and you're not allowed to eat a bag of crisps or a doughnut? They'd rather you just collapsed in a heap? If someone's child fell under a bus through being weak from hunger and not allowed to eat, their parents could probably sue the school. That's what I'd have thought. But Skye is a bit of a boffin, she likes to get good marks and be well thought of. Not that she is a teacher's pet, or anything; she is just a natural straight-A student. She is the only person I have ever known who actually *enjoys* doing her SATS. You can never tell what people are going to like or not like; we are all different. Me and Jem have learnt to accept it. You can't help the way your brain is wired.

"We'll give her one more minute," said Skye. "Starting from… *now.*"

She stood, watching the second hand go ticking round the dial. She is always very precise.

I said, "Know what I think?"

"What?"

"I think she only said it was her favourite cos of wanting to get me into trouble."

"What are you talking about?" said Skye.

"*Angel*. Saying it was her favourite shirt. She only said it cos of m—"

"Do we have to?" said Skye. "I thought you weren't going to talk about it any more?"

"Well, I wasn't. But I bet if she hadn't discovered it she wouldn't even have remembered she'd got it."

"Yeah, yeah," said Skye. "Right, that's it! We're going."

She shot off on stilt-like legs up the road. I practically had to run to keep up with her.

"She has some nerve," I said. "I mean, when does she ever do anything to help? All she ever does is wash her hair and paint her nails and—"

"Oi!" We stopped, and turned. A small huffing figure was scurrying towards us. "You could have waited," it said.

"We did wait," said Skye. "You're late."

"Only a few minutes. Don't go on at me!"

"Talk about going on," I said. "You should have heard my sister."

Skye groaned. "Not again!"

"She's going to burst a blood vessel one of these days if she's not careful."

Jem said, "Yeah?" And then, in this slightly hysterical tone of voice, "Don't talk to me! I don't want to know!"

"She shrivelled her shirt," said Skye. "I've had to hear all about it, why shouldn't you?"

"Cos if anyone talks to me," said Jem, "I shall be the one that bursts a blood vessel. I don't want to know, I don't want to know!" She stuffed her fingers in her ears. "Just don't talk to me!"

"No problem," I said. "We can easily pretend you're not here. You just hang back and—" I broke off. "Excuse me?" I turned, politely. "Did you wish to say something? Or was that a mouse squeaking?"

"*Why* did you shrivel her shirt?" said Jem.

Skye gave a muffled scream. "Don't ask!"

"I thought you wanted me to hear?"

"I've changed my mind. Anyway, you said you didn't want anyone talking to you."

"I don't," said Jem. "I feel like I'm going to explode. Like the top of my skull's going to burst open." She brought her hand down, *whumpff*, on top of her head.

"That's right," said Skye, kindly. "You keep hold of it."

Jem made a noise that sounded like *aaargh* and went beetling off ahead, her legs (which aren't very long) pumping up and down, her hand still clamped to her head.

It might, I suppose, be considered cause for alarm, our best friend saying she was about to explode; but me and Skye have known Jem for too long. She is one of those up-and-down sort of people. All fizzing and bubbling one minute, then pop! The cork comes flying out of the bottle and she's, like, climbing the walls. Or holding her head on. It's impossible to keep up with her. At least with Angel you *know* she's going to be in a rage, cos she practically lives in one. With Jem it's like being on a mad rollercoaster.

"Fizzy Pop," I said. I turned to Skye. "D'you remember? That's what we used to call her."

"That was when Mrs Fletcher told her she ought to calm down or she'd burst."

"It was a good name," I said. "Why did we stop using it?"

"You decided nicknames were naff."

"*I* did?"

"Yes, you didn't like being called Rumblebelly."

"Oh. Well," I said, "that was just rude. And it only happened once! Jem's like fizzing and popping all the time."

We both gazed at her small scurrying

figure. She'd stopped holding her head on, but she was still whizzing along at an absurdly fast rate.

"Let's get a move on," said Skye. "I don't want to miss registration!"

First period that day was geography with Mr Harper, who likes to drone on about rift valleys and things and never notices what people get up to so long as they get up to it quietly and don't disturb anyone who might just want to hear what he's saying.

Me and Jem sat in the back row, with Skye between us. Skye really likes to pay attention in class, so she wasn't best pleased when Jem pushed a note in front of her and pointed at me. She thinks it is childish to pass notes. Impatiently, not taking her eyes off Mr Harper, she flicked the note towards me.

y U shrivel shirt?

I sent a note back: *Not my fault. y U think*

skull going 2 burst?

Tell U ltr, replied Jem. *Y not yr fault?*

I was about to explain about the iron, and all the electricity rushing out of control through the mains, but I didn't get the chance because at that point Skye wrote *STOP IT! BEHAVE YOURSELVES,* heavily underlined, on the back of her geography book.

She can't help being bossy; both her mum and dad are teachers.

Second period was English with Miss Rolfe, who gave us back the essays we'd written the previous week on the subject of 'Beginnings'. We'd had to write all about our early lives, as much as we could remember.

"On the whole," said Miss Rolfe, "I was quite pleased with them." Ooh! It takes a lot to please Miss Rolfe. "Daisy, could you hand these back for me? There is one that I would really love to read aloud… Jemma?"

Jem looked startled. She is not used to

being singled out, unless it's for talking, or fidgeting, or not paying attention.

"Do I have your permission?" said Miss Rolfe. "I won't if you'd rather I didn't."

Jem by now was bright pillar-box red. "It's OK," she muttered.

"Are you sure? Maybe you'd like to read it yourself?"

Jem shook her head, violently.

"All right, then. Here we go! This is what Jemma wrote.

"*My beginnings are shrouded in mystery as I was adopted when I was a baby and don't remember anything about my life before. Some people feel sorry for me and say it must be terrible not ever having known my real mum and dad, but as far as I am concerned my mum and dad that adopted me are my real mum and dad. I don't want any others! Maybe one day I will feel curious and want to know who my birth mother was but for the moment I am* perfectly happy and anyway I would not like to upset Mum and Dad by trying to find out in case they might think I didn't love them.

"One of the things about being adopted is that people never say to you, 'Oh, don't you look like your mum?' which is what they sometimes say to my friends that aren't adopted and my friends get really mad as for some reason they don't seem to want to look like their mums. My mum is quite large and jolly and laughs a lot. I am rather small and not always jolly, though I do like to have a bit of a laugh. Dad is very sweet and gentle, and that is definitely not like me! I am sure if you asked my friends they would say that sweet and gentle is the last thing I am!!! I am not sure what they would say I was. A bit of a pain, probably.

"I am an only child, and only children are often said to be spoilt, but I don't think my mum and dad spoil me. Mum is quite strict in *spite of being jolly. Dad is not quite so strict as he tends to leave all the telling-off to Mum, but if she says NO he always backs her up. I feel very grateful to them for adopting me. I'm sure there were lots of other babies they could have had if they'd wanted. I think that is the BEST thing about being adopted, you know that you have been chosen and it makes you feel special."*

There was a silence as Miss Rolfe finished reading; then Skye started to clap, and all the rest of us joined in. It was so amazing! It was obvious that everyone was really moved by what Jem had written. It was just such a brave thing to do. It made me feel quite ashamed of my own essay, which had gone on at great length about Angel and her temper, and Tom being an alien. I'd never once thought to say that I loved Mum and Dad. *Or* Rags. Or even Angel and Tom, if it came to that. Cos I do love them, in spite of everything. I would just have been too embarrassed to say so.

"I think you'll agree," said Miss Rolfe, "that that was really heart-warming. Refreshingly honest. Thank you very much, Jemma, for letting me read it. Girls, I know that was the bell, but please don't rush!"

Me and Skye wandered slowly out into the playground with Jem, who was still quite pink.

"That was brilliant," said Skye.

I said, "Yes, it was. "

I thought Jem would be pleased, but instead she looked at us with her face all scrunched up and said, "Oh, I *wish* she hadn't done that!"

CHAPTER THREE

"Done what?" said Skye.

"Read it out!"

"But it was lovely," I said.

"*Refreshingly honest.*"

"And heart-warming!"

"It could even get chosen for Speech Day," said Skye.

We'd been told by Miss Rolfe that every year one junior girl and one senior girl got to read out their essays in front of the whole school, including parents and governors, not to mention what she called "local dignitaries". Meaning the Mayor, I suppose, and the Mayor's husband. It is hard to think what other dignitaries there could be.

"Imagine," said Skye, "you'd have your picture in the paper."

"I don't want my picture in the paper!"

Pardon me? Was this my friend Jem speaking? Just last term at primary school we'd had an author visit and Jem had been the first to rush forward when the photographs were taken. She'd been so eager she'd practically left a trail of bodies behind her. I reminded her of this and she said, "That was different."

I said, "How?"

"It just was!"

"Is it because you don't want people knowing you're adopted? Cos that's just silly! Like you wrote in your essay, being adopted makes you special."

"You think so?" said Jem.

"Well, that's what you wrote! Anyway, you didn't have to let her read it. You could have said no."

"Didn't like to," muttered Jem.

"But why would you want to?" Skye was obviously at a loss. She is always having her stuff read out. "It's an honour!"

Jem sighed. "I s'pose."

"So what is the problem?" We'd reached our favourite corner of the playground, hidden away in the angle between the drama studio and the wall which separates us from Tom's school next door. We'd staked it out as our territory from the word go. It was a bit dark and dingy, but it was where we went when we wanted to be private. "I don't get it," said Skye. "I mean... heart-warming!"

"Refreshingly honest."

"But it's not true!" wailed Jem.

Not true? Was she telling us she *wasn't* adopted?

"When you say not true… which bits," said Skye, "exactly?"

"The yucky stuff."

"You mean, like, about your mum?"

"All that stuff about her being jolly and Dad being sweet and me being perfectly happy… all *yuck*!"

We stared at her, perplexed.

"Has someone upset you, or something?" said Skye.

"Mum, if you must know!"

"Your mum?" What could she have done? Me and Skye adore Jem's mum. She *is* large and jolly, and she does laugh a lot. She's fun!

"What's she done?" said Skye.

"Just gone and ruined my entire life is all!"

Uh-oh! Me and Skye looked at each other. I pulled a face: Skye rolled her eyes. It is hard, sometimes, to take Jem seriously, especially when she goes into drama queen mode. But we are her friends and she was obviously desperate to offload. Now that the cork was out of the bottle, there was no stopping her. Her mum was impossible! She didn't understand her, she didn't even try to understand her. And her dad just sat on the fence. He never stood up for her! He never even stood up for himself.

"He just agrees with everything Mum says! It doesn't matter what it is, she's the boss and he just goes along with it. Like *ask your mum* and *what does your mum say?* and—"

"And what does she say?" said Skye.

"She says no! So Dad says no!"

"Says no to what? I'm afraid," said Skye, "you are not making any sense. Try starting at the beginning," she said kindly, "then perhaps we'll know what you're talking about."

"Right." Jem heaved a great quivering sigh and clutched at her hair with both hands.

I wondered if the top of her skull was coming off again. "There's this girl in my road? Liliana? She's, like, thirteen?"

We nodded, solemnly.

"Well, she's joined this model agency, OK? And she's already got her first job, modelling clothes for a catalogue, and they're paying her, like, a *fortune*? So she says why don't I enrol, cos they're really looking for kids like me, sort of… " Jem waved a hand.

"Pretty," I said. I don't mind admitting that Jem is pretty.

"Yes. Well, sort of. But, like, good in front of a camera. You know?"

Jem *is* good in front of a camera. It's why she loves being photographed. Me and Skye just freeze, but Jem really plays to it.

"So anyway," she said, "I asked Mum if I could sign up, I *begged* her to let me. I *pleaded* with her! I told her I would *so* like to be a model, cos I feel it's something

I could really do. You know?"

"I thought you wanted to be a make-up artist," said Skye.

"There's nothing to stop me being both! I could be a model *and* a make-up artist. This girl, Liliana? She says it's so cool! She's even got her own portfolio."

I said, "What's a portfolio?"

"It's like this collection of photos? Like head-and-shoulders and full-length... all different. But big ones! Not just titchy little things. You get them when you join the agency."

"What, for free?"

"Well... sort of. You don't have to pay them till you start earning money. But Liliana's already earning money! Her mum's putting it in the building society for her, for when she's older. If I did that, it would help me go to college to study make-up and stuff. I told Mum, I said it would mean she and Dad wouldn't have to pay anything, but she wouldn't listen. She's just so… *stodgy*. And fat! She's *fat*. That's why she won't let me do it! She doesn't approve of people being models. She thinks they're too thin. She hates people that are thin! She says what I do when I leave school is up to me, but she's not having me starving myself to a size zero while I'm in her care. Like I would! She's just being totally *stupid*. And all Dad says is, *it's up to your mum*. It's all he ever says!"

On she went; on and on. We did our best to console her. I made soothing noises and Skye made what I think were supposed to be helpful suggestions such as, "Maybe if she sees you're really serious your mum will change her mind," and, "Maybe you should speak to your dad and tell him how much it means to you." So Skye! But Jem had gone into tragic mode. We obviously didn't understand: her life had been blighted! Totally blighted!

This other girl, Liliana, was going to get rich and famous while Jem would be left behind to moulder. All because of her mum!

I did sort of feel sympathetic, cos I know what's it's like to desperately want to do something and not be allowed to. Like one time when I really really *really* wanted to try hang gliding and Mum said, "At your age? You must be joking!" and Dad said, not on your life. I sulked for a while, like about a day or two, but then something else turned up and I forgot about it. I could see that not being allowed to join a modelling agency was probably more frustrating for Jem than me not being allowed to go hang gliding, since hang gliding wasn't exactly going to turn into a full-time career. Jem really could be a model. Well, a mini model. As Skye somewhat tactlessly pointed out, she wasn't ever likely to grow tall enough to be a proper one.

I groaned. That was *absolutely* the wrong

thing to say. That just got her going even more. She kept at it all the rest of the day. All through the lunch hour, all through the afternoon break, all the way home. It's funny how some people can't ever let a subject drop.

I wondered, as we all peeled off in our different directions, what Mum would say if I told her I wanted to do modelling. Not that I did, I am just like totally the wrong shape, being sort of… square, I suppose is the word. But I thought I would put it to her, just out of interest. See if she reacted the same way as Jem's mum. If she did, then maybe it would make Jem feel a bit better and not so down on poor Mrs McClusky. It was really mean of her to call her mum fat!

I started to yell "*Mu-u-um*" as soon as I let myself in, but then I saw that the door of the front room was closed which meant Mum had someone in there so I went through to the kitchen to find that Dad was home. He was sitting at the kitchen table with Angel, eating pizza. Well, Dad was eating pizza; Angel was nibbling on a lettuce leaf. I was glad he was there as there was something I'd been meaning to ask him. It was a pity about Angel, but as she lives in the same house it is not always easy to avoid her.

"Dad," I said.

Dad said, "Mm?"

"Can you tell me something?"

"Don't know till you ask."

"If you were using an iron," I said, "and all of a sudden there was a power s—"

"Not again!" shouted Angel. "Don't you ever give up?"

She looked like she might be going to turn violent.

"Well, all right, then," I said. "What about the garden shed? You don't th—"

Angel screamed. A short, sharp, mad sort of scream.

"Do you mind?" I said. "I'm trying to talk."

"Yes, and I'm trying to relax," said Dad. "Do I have to remind you both that I was out of the house by five thirty this morning? I've had a hard day, I can do without you two going at each other."

There was a pause.

"I've had a hard day," I said. "We had double maths after lunch."

"Shut up," said Angel.

"Shut up yourself!"

"No, you shut up!"

Dad banged on the table. Tom, who had silently come in and helped himself to a slice of pizza, went silently back out. At the door he bumped into Mum, on her way in.

"What's going on?" said Mum. "What's with all the noise?"

"They're at it again," said Tom.

"For goodness' sake!" Mum pulled out a chair and sat down next to Dad. "If you have to shout, go and do it somewhere else. Not down our ears!"

Very dignified, cos I wasn't going to lower myself to Angel's level, I said, "Pardon me, but I was just trying to talk."

"Just trying to make excuses! Drivelling on about power surges. Honestly," said Angel, "I sometimes can't believe I'm related to it. You didn't secretly adopt it or something, did you?"

"Not as far as I can recall," said Mum.

"It wouldn't worry me," I said. "Jem's adopted. She says it makes you special. But I think if I was," I said, "I'd want to find out who my birth mother was. Wouldn't you?"

"I suppose I might, at some stage," agreed Mum.

"Jem says she's not interested." Well, that's what she'd said in her essay. She might feel differently now that her life had been blighted. "She says she wouldn't want her mum and dad thinking she didn't love them."

"In that case," said Mum, "don't you go putting ideas in her head."

"Me?" I said.

"Yes, you."

"I wouldn't!"

"Well, make sure you don't."

I munched for a bit on a slice of pizza.

"Jem wants to join a model agency," I said. "She's decided she wants to model clothes for catalogues and earn pots of money. Would you let one of us do that? If we wanted to? Jem's mum won't let her. Jem's so upset."

"I wouldn't mind joining a model agency," said Angel.

"Oh, no!" Mum was very firm about it. "We're having none of that, young woman! You're already quite obsessed enough with your weight as it is."

"So you mean you wouldn't let us?" I said. "Not even me? I'm not obsessed!"

"Neither of you," said Mum.

"But why not? I don't understand why not!"

"Because apart from anything else, it would distract from your school work."

"And who would want you, anyway?" said Angel.

I said, "Somebody might."

Angel tossed her head. She likes doing that as it makes her hair swish. I guess she thinks it will attract boys.

"You have to be joking," she said. "What would you model? Boxing gloves?"

Dad banged again on the table. "Enough!" he said. "I have had enough. If you can't manage to be civilised with each other—"

I said, "I'm civilised. She was the one being rude."

Angel opened her mouth, then caught Dad's eye and closed it again. Dad doesn't very often get ratty, but when he does it's best not to try his patience.

"I'm going up to my room," I said, grabbing a slice of pizza.

"Good," said Angel. "Give us all a break."

I hope Dad told her off. If he didn't, he so should! She is the rudest person on earth.

Next morning, on the way to school, I told Jem about Mum saying how she wouldn't let either me or Angel do modelling.

"So you see it's not just your mum," I said. "It's mine, as well."

I'd hoped Jem would find this a comfort and stop raging on about her mum being prejudiced against thin people, but all it did was start her off all over again.

"*Specially chosen*," she said. "Huh! They probably just took what they could get. *Here's a baby nobody wants, have this one!*"

"What makes you think nobody wanted you?" said Skye.

"Wouldn't have been up for adoption otherwise, would I?"

"Doesn't mean nobody *wanted* you."

"Means my real mum didn't."

I said, "Your real mum? I thought you s—"

"My *birth* mum!"

"Well, but you don't actually know," I said. "You don't know anything about her. Just cos she had you adopted doesn't necessarily mean she didn't want you."

Jem looked at me, doubtfully.

"She could have been forced into it. You just don't know."

Jem said, "Mm… maybe."

"Anything could have happened! They could have come and torn you away from her, and she'd be like all screaming and crying… *don't take my baby! Don't let them take my baby!*"

I clutched, dramatically, at an imaginary bundle. A woman passing by gave me a very odd stare.

"They do these things," I said. Jem's eyes had gone like saucers. "They're always snatching people's babies!"

"What she means," said Skye, "is they might have thought she couldn't cope."

"My mum couldn't cope?"

"Yes, like if she was a dr—" Skye stopped.

"Like if she was *what*?" said Jem.

"Oh!" Skye waved a hand. "You know… like if she was still at school, or something."

Jem looked at her, uncertainly. I went rushing in to the rescue. "She wouldn't have *wanted* to give you up. She probably loved you to bits! She could be wondering even now where you are and what you're doing… praying that you're all right. Weeping on your birthday… "

Jem put a finger in her mouth and chewed, hesitantly, at a fingernail. Even Skye seemed moved by the tragic picture I was painting. I was moved myself. I could see it all so clearly! A pale young woman, the tears streaming down her cheeks as she struggled desperately to hold on to her baby. Omigod, it was heart-rending!

Jem took her finger out of her mouth. "Stop it," she said. "I can't bear it!"

"It's only a scenario," said Skye. She tends to use these sort of words. "We don't know that it's actually what happened."

"But it could be," choked Jem. "My mum, she could be out there, worrying about me!" And she stuffed her finger back in her mouth and began nibbling, furiously, like a rabbit.

"If it bothers you that much," I said, "maybe—"

"What, what?" spluttered Jem.

"Maybe you should see if you can find her?"

CHAPTER FOUR

I didn't mean to say it. I didn't do it on purpose! The words just slipped out, as words do; you can't always control them. I find this happens quite a lot. Mum says it is what comes of being over-eager and not stopping to think before I speak. But I think and speak at the same time! It is just the way I am made, I have these very quick reactions.

Jem had taken her finger back out of her mouth and come to a full stop in the middle of the street. She was looking at me, searchingly.

"You really think that's what I ought to do? Try and trace my real mum?"

"Your *birth* mum." Mrs McClusky was her real mum.

"You really think I should?" said Jem.

"Well… only if it's what you feel." I wasn't going to push her, cos that would be wrong.

"I don't know!" wailed Jem.

We were nearly at the school gates.

"Think about it," said Skye. "We'll discuss it later."

"I've decided." Jem hissed it at us as we went into the playground at break. "I'm going to do it!"

"Are you sure?" said Skye. She sounded a bit anxious, though I couldn't think why. It seemed to me anyone that had been adopted would want to find their birth mother. It wasn't anything to do with not loving their *real* mum, it was just ordinary, natural, human curiosity. Well, that's what I would have thought. But Skye is a very cautious sort of person; she doesn't believe in rushing headlong into things. She likes to weigh them up and make mental lists like For and Against. Me and Jem can't be bothered with all that; we tend to go more on impulse.

"It's a big decision," said Skye.

"I know." Jem said it very solemnly. "I've been thinking about it all morning." All through French, all through history… she'd been told off twice for not paying attention. "The only thing is…" She hesitated. "Where do I start?"

"Ask your mum?" said Skye.

"I can't ask Mum! I know I'm like totally *furious* with her, but she might think I was doing it to pay her back, kind of thing. I wouldn't want her thinking that! Cos honestly, I'm not."

Jem said it earnestly. I agreed.

"You're doing it cos you want to *know*. It's your right."

"How about asking your dad?" said Skye.

Jem made a scoffing sound. "No use asking *him*. He'd just say, ask your mum. Then he'd go and tell her, and she'd get all hurt and stuff."

I was glad Jem didn't want her mum to be hurt. But all the same, it *was* her right. There had to be some way she could find out.

"There's got to be records," I said.

"But where?"

We both turned, instinctively, to Skye. She is a mine of information about all sorts of things, like if you want to know the capital of Peru or how far away the sun is from the earth. But Skye shrugged her shoulders and said she didn't know.

"In some government office, maybe?"

I made a face. That wasn't any good. Government offices wouldn't tell you anything; specially not if you were only eleven years old. There'd be bound to be some kind of law against it.

"P'raps when you were adopted," I said, "there'd have been papers or something?" I was a bit vague about what kind of papers, but it seems to me there are papers for pretty well everything. Dad always complains that he is drowning in them. He says, "Papers for this, papers for that… it's a wonder there are any trees left standing."

"You could always try looking," I said.

"I could." Jem brightened. "I know where they'd be… in Mum and Dad's desk. They keep everything in there, all locked away. The key's in their dressing-table drawer. I can easily get it. It's just a question of waiting for the right moment."

"You mean like when your mum and dad aren't there." Skye had that look she sometimes gets, with her mouth all pursed, like she's sucking on lemons. "This is starting to sound a bit off, if you ask me. It's like you're spying on them."

I said, "She's not spying on them! She's just trying to find out something she's got every right to know, only she doesn't want to hurt her mum."

"I wouldn't read anything that's private," said Jem. "I'm only looking for stuff that's about me."

Skye's lips were still pursed. She can be *so* exasperating!

"If you won't even let her look," I said, "how is she supposed to find out?"

"I'm not sure finding out is such a good idea," said Skye.

"But it's her right!"

"It's my right," said Jem.

"It's all very well keeping on saying that, but suppose when you find out you wish you hadn't?"

Jem scrunched her face into a frown. "Why would I wish that?"

"You might find something you don't like! People do," said Skye. "They have these fantasies their mums are going to be celebs, or royalty, or something, and then they turn out to be… I don't know! Something not very nice."

I said, "*Some* people find their mums are celebs. Or their dads," I added.

In wondering tones, Jem said, "I never thought about my dad."

"You can think about him later," I told her. "The important thing is to find your mum."

"You're right!" She nodded. "I'll find her first, then I can ask her about my dad."

I said, "Yes, cos she'll be able to tell you who he was."

"Maybe," said Skye. "Maybe not."

We both rounded on her. "Don't be so negative!" I said.

"It's not going to stop me," said Jem. "I'm still going to do it, I don't care what you say. I want to find out!"

Jem and Skye were waiting for me on the corner next morning. Eagerly, I went racing up to them.

"What happened? Did you find anything?"

"Haven't been able to look yet," said Jem.

"Give her a chance!" Skye biffed me with her school bag. "It's not easy, being a spy. You can't just go blundering into things."

"Mum and Dad are always there," explained Jem.

My mum and dad are always there, but I felt sure I could creep into their bedroom without them knowing. Well, I had done! On lots of occasions. Searching for Christmas presents on top of the wardrobe...

"It's all right for you," said Jem. "You don't live in a flat."

That was true. I could see that being all on one floor might make things a bit difficult. In a house you can disappear upstairs and nobody knows which room you're in, but Jem's place is quite small and her mum and dad's bedroom is right next door to the sitting room.

"I'll do it as soon as I can," said Jem.

I said, "That's OK. I won't ask you again until… this time next week!"

"Like we believe *that*?" said Skye. "Come on, you two! Get a move on."

Skye went power-walking off, leaving me and Jem to trail behind.

"I'll do it before next week," said Jem. "I promise!"

I pointed out that she wasn't doing it for *me*. "It's *your* birth mum. You're the one that needs to know!"

Every morning after that I looked at her, hopefully, but didn't actually say anything. It took a *lot* of self-control. I couldn't help this sneaking feeling that if a person really, seriously wanted to do something, they would find a way of doing it. I would! But maybe that is just me.

The weekend came and went. So did Monday. On Tuesday when I gave my hopeful look Jem said, "I nearly went and blew it! Dad was having a bath and Mum was in the kitchen so I took a chance and guess what? Mum came into the bedroom and found me there!"

I said, "Wow."

"You can say wow," said Skye. "You weren't the one being caught red-handed!"

I looked anxiously at Jem. "Were you really?"

"Not quite," said Jem, "but it was a nasty moment."

"What did you say?"

"I told Mum I was looking for Titch."

Titch is her hamster. I nodded. "That was quick thinking."

"Spies have to be quick," said Skye.

"Shut up about spies! She's not spying."

"I'm beginning to feel like I am," said Jem. "But I'm not giving up!"

That was the day Miss Rolfe announced that Jem's essay on Beginnings had been chosen for Speech Day. I could tell from the way Jem's cheeks fired up that she was pleased and proud, but also a bit embarrassed.

"All that yucky stuff," she wailed later, to me and Skye.

"People like yucky stuff," said Skye.

"I know, but it doesn't feel right… not when I'm planning to go through Mum and Dad's private papers behind their back!"

"In that case maybe you shouldn't be doing it." Skye looked hard at Jem.

"What? You mean…" Jem paused, uncertain. "Reading out my essay?"

"No! Going through your mum and dad's stuff."

"But I need to know!"

"It's her right," I said.

"It may be her right, but if it's going to make her feel bad… why don't you just *talk* to them?"

"I can't!" Jem shook her head. "You know I can't!"

"You're still cross with your mum," I said.

She wasn't in quite such a sulk as she had been, though every now and again she would remember that she had a grievance and start going on about being misunderstood and her life being blighted, so I could see it probably wasn't a good time for her to start asking questions.

"I think, personally," said Skye, "you should just wait."

I said, "Wait for what?"

"Wait till she's back to normal with her mum, then she can sit down and have a talk."

"How can I ever be back to normal," shrilled Jem, "when every minute that ticks past is another minute of my life *wasted*? Liliana's just done a photo shoot for the Teen Scene catalogue and she's threatening to bring it round and *show* it to me!"

In spite of being so maddeningly sensible, Skye does seem to have the knack of always saying the wrong thing.

"Now look what you've done," I hissed. "Just as she was starting to get over it!"

I knew straight away, the next morning, that Jem had something to report. She was jigging up and down with impatience.

"I did it, I did it! I found something!"

"What, what?"

"Tell!"

Even Skye could hardly contain herself.

"You found her?" I yelled. "You found your birth mum?"

"No, but I've found something… I've found that I was *discovered*," said Jem.

"Discovered how?" I said.

"Discovered where?" said Skye.

"On the steps of a church…" Jem announced it in a ghostly whisper. "Left in the churchyard, wrapped in a shawl… "

I was about to say "Wow" but stopped myself just in time.

"How did you find out?" said Skye.

"I waited till Mum and Dad had gone upstairs to this residents' meeting, then I crept into the bedroom and got the key and went back to the sitting room and—"

"Yes, yes, we know all that," said Skye.

"Just get on with it!" I said.

Jem looked hurt. "I'm setting the scene."

"But what did you *find*?"

"I found this cutting from a newspaper… all old and yellow. All about this tiny baby that had been abandoned."

"And that was you?"

"It has to be," said Jem, "or why would they have kept it?"

74

"What was the date?" said Skye.

"Dunno." Jem crinkled her nose. "That bit was torn off. But it did say it was lucky I was discovered in time cos it was one of the coldest February days for decades!"

Jem's birthday is in February. We stared at her, in a kind of awe. She had been in the paper!

"You should have brought it with you," I said. "We might have been able to find things out."

"Like what?"

"Well … like which paper it was?"

"That wouldn't help her find her birth mum," said Skye.

"No, but at least she'd know if it was local."

"It was," said Jem. Her cheeks glowed, pinkly. "It said St Peter's. You know where that is? Down Old Town, near the Arcade!"

This time I did say wow. The Arcade! We all knew where that was. We used to beg our mums to take us there when we were little so we could go on the roundabout and ride on the toy train. To think we'd been only minutes away from where Jem had been abandoned…

"Know what?" I said. "We ought to go down there and have a look!"

Jem's face lit up. "Shall we?" She turned to Skye. "Shall we do that?"

I waited for Skye to read us one of her lectures and tell us why it was a bad idea and we shouldn't go, but for once she seemed quite enthusiastic.

"OK," she said. "Why not? We could meet up Saturday afternoon and take the tram to Old Town. It'll be like a kind of pilgrimage."

"Oh, this is so exciting!" Jem clasped her hands to her chest; her eyes were glowing. "It's the most exciting thing that's ever happened to me!"

CHAPTER
FIVE

"It's like a sort of pilgrimage," I said.

It was Saturday afternoon and I was waiting for Jem and Skye. Mum was in the front room putting the finishing touches to something green and glittery. Getting a bit sidetracked, I said, "That's pretty!"

"It is, isn't it?" said Mum. She shook it out and held it up for me to see. All the spangles twinkled and shone.

"What is it?" I said.

"It's for Emilia… Mrs Duffy's little girl. For her Book Week. She's going as a dewdrop."

I said, "Blimey!"

An expression of annoyance crossed Mum's face. "What do you mean, *blimey*? What is that supposed to mean?"

I backed off, hastily. "It's what Dad says."

"Well, there's no call for you to say it."

"It's not rude," I said.

Mum tightened her lips.

"It's not! Honestly! I asked Dad. It just means, God blind me if I tell a lie… or something. It got shortened. But that's all it means!"

"What it means," said Mum, "is that you're being snotty about poor little Emilia dressing up as a dewdrop."

"Mum, she's *thirteen*. She has *learning difficulties*."

"Yes, and this is what she's set her heart on. Just let her have her moment."

"But people will laugh at her!"

"Nobody is going to laugh at her."

"B—"

"Frankie, I do know what I'm doing! I've been at this a long time. Just let it be."

Honestly! She didn't have to get all offended. I was only trying to help.

"What's this pilgrimage you're going on?"

"We're going to the Arcade." I tugged at a bit of twig that was tangled in Rags's fur. "Down Old Town."

"Good heavens," said Mum. "That's a trip down memory lane. I wonder if the children's playground is still there?"

"Dunno," I said. "We're not going for that. We're going to look at a church… St *Peter's*. We're going to look at the steps." I yanked at another bit of twig. Rags seemed to have brought half the park home with him.

"Why would you want to look at steps?" said Mum.

I'd been hoping she'd ask me that.

"Cos Jem's just discovered," I said, "that that's where she was found… wrapped in a shawl, on the steps of the church. *Abandoned*. All those years ago!"

"Really?" said Mum. "Who told her that?"

"She read it in this old newspaper cutting. She was looking through some papers in her mum and dad's desk and she came across it."

Mum paused. "It was you," she said, "wasn't it? You put her up to it!"

I was indignant. "I so didn't!"

"Then why was she looking through her mum and dad's papers?"

"Well, cos she was hoping to find out about her birth mum. It was her idea!" I said. "Sort of."

"*Sort* of." Mum snipped off a bit of thread between her teeth. "You just couldn't resist it, could you? You had to go and meddle!"

"She's very unhappy," I said. "She reckons her life has been blighted."

"All because she's not allowed to join a modelling agency?"

"It means a lot to her."

"So now she's trying to trace her birth mother?" Mum shook her head. "I just hope it doesn't all end in disaster."

Honestly! Mum was as bad as Skye. Why did they always have to look on the black side? Why couldn't they imagine *nice* things happening?

"Her mum doesn't have to have been someone bad," I said. "She could turn out to be rich and famous!"

"And Jem could end up feeling resentful and dissatisfied."

I said, "She already does."

"She'd get over it. Really, Frankie, I don't know why you just can't leave well alone. Why must you keep interfering all the time?"

I felt really hurt when she said that. "I wasn't interfering," I said. "Jem's my friend! I was trying to help."

"But we had all this out," said Mum. "You promised you wouldn't go putting ideas into her head. And stop plucking and picking at that dog! We don't want hairs all over the place."

"I'm cleaning him up," I said. Only five minutes earlier Mum had been complaining that he was all matted and covered in bits of park. "I'm only trying t—"

"I know, I know," said Mum. "You're only trying to help! It's good that you're cleaning him, but why not do the job properly while you're about it? With his brush – in the garden. Not in here when I have someone coming!"

There is just no pleasing some people. It wasn't like I'd have left all the bits of twig on the floor; I'd have got the dustpan and brush and swept them up! I didn't want to do him in the garden cos Angel was out there, with some of her friends. They were all shrieking and painting their nails with black nail varnish. Fingers *and* toes. Chances were, if she saw me, she'd only start on about something. She still hadn't forgiven me for crinkling her shirt.

"Can we do it in the kitchen?" I said.

"I'd rather you didn't," said Mum. "You know what happened last time."

"That was cos someone had left the lid off the cake tin!"

All Mum's cakes had been covered in dog hair. But it wasn't my fault! *I* hadn't left the lid off. Not as far as I could remember.

"Frankie, just humour me," said Mum. "Just for once. The garden is the place for brushing dogs, not the kitchen."

I still wasn't going out there. I didn't see why I should be expected to suffer a mouthful of abuse when all I was doing was just trying to help. Like *Angel* ever does anything. Or Tom, for that matter.

"I'll take him up to my bedroom," I said.

I opened the door and Rags shot out. There was an immediate bellow from Dad: "Keep that dog away!" I'd forgotten, Dad was painting the skirting board, all up the stairs. He was having to do it, he said, cos of the number of times I'd whacked it with my hockey stick or bounced balls off it, throwing them for Rags. I get blamed for everything in our house.

I led Rags up the stairs *most* carefully, not going anywhere near the skirting board. I couldn't be bothered fetching his brush from the kitchen so I used my own. I am not one of those people that are neurotic about a bit of dog hair.

"Good boy," I said. "Good *boy!*"

While I was brushing him I heard the front door bell.

"That'll be Jem and Skye," I said.

I scrambled to my feet and rushed out on to the landing. Rags rushed with me. Oops! I'd completely forgotten about the skirting board…

"FRANKIE FOSTER, I'LL HAVE YOUR GUTS FOR GARTERS!" roared Dad.

Hastily, I crammed myself out of the front door and slammed it behind me.

"Who was that?" Jem giggled. "Was it your dad?" I don't know what she found so funny about it. A father threatening to have his daughter's guts for garters? That's child abuse, that is.

"What did you do?" said Skye.

"Didn't do anything," I said. "It was Rags, touching his paintwork."

"So why's he having a go at you?"

"They always have a go at me."

"*Aaaaah.*" Skye made a crooning noise. She patted my head, consolingly. "It's so not fair!"

"It so isn't," I said. They never have a go at Tom or Angel.

"Never mind all that. We're on a pilgrimage!"

Jem went skipping off ahead of us. "A pilgrimage, we're on a pilgrimage!"

I do like it when she's happy, but it is somewhat embarrassing when she starts dancing and twirling in the middle of the street. I guess it's one reason she would have made a good model; she doesn't care who sees her.

"Stop fizzing and popping," said Skye. "This is a serious quest."

Was it? I supposed it was. After all, it's not every day a person gets to gaze upon the very spot they were abandoned as a tiny baby.

"It's like visiting a shrine," I said.

We caught the tram at the top of the road and went trundling off to Old Town. There's a big supermarket down there, right next to the Arcade, which is where we used to go on the toy train when we were little.

"Oh! Look," I cried, as we got off. "The train's still there!"

But Jem wasn't interested in the train; she was anxious to get to the shrine. I could understand her impatience. This was a big moment for her.

"So what exactly are we looking for?" said Skye.

"Market Square. The church is just off it. I looked it up on the map, it must be…" Jem pointed, rather wildly. "That way!"

"That's the bus garage," said Skye.

"All right, then… that way?"

"That goes down to the canal. You haven't got the faintest idea," said Skye, "have you?"

"But I looked it up!"

Skye regarded her, pityingly. "You know you have no sense of direction," she said. Jem had once famously got lost between our classroom and the toilets at primary school. They were both on the same corridor! "I'd better go and ask or we'll be here all day."

"I looked it up," whimpered Jem.

I told her not to worry. "I expect you're in a bit of a state."

Jem admitted that she was. "I've been looking forward to this all week!"

"It is a historic event," I said.

Market Square turned out to be on the opposite side of the main road leading out of town. It's a three-lane highway, crammed with container lorries and huge great trucks. Quite scary. Skye told Jem to "Wait for the lights and *don't go rushing off,*" like she was a child. But Jem accepted it meekly; I think she was starting to feel a bit anxious.

We reached Market Square at last, and there was the church. Very old and forbidding, with a scrubby patch of graveyard and a few crumbly graves. And there, right ahead of us, were the steps. Jem stopped, transfixed. Like she couldn't tear her eyes away.

"Course, this is daytime," I said. "It would have been night time, probably, when she left you here. I can just picture it… creeping up, holding you in her arms—" I clutched again at my imaginary bundle. "Looking all round to make sure no one could see her. Giving you one last kiss… mwah!" My lips brushed the air. "Then laying you down ever so gently at the top of the steps."

"Why not in the porch?" said Skye.

"Cos she wouldn't have been able to get in!" Really, Skye has *no* imagination. "Not at dead of night. The doors would've been locked. She'd probably have laid you just *here*—" Very carefully, I knelt and set down my bundle. "Here, in the corner, so's you'd be sheltered."

Jem suddenly raced past me, hurled herself on to the top step and curled into a ball.

"What are you doing?" cried Skye.

"I'm being me, as a baby! I'm trying to feel what it must have been like."

"Cold, I reckon. What time did they discover you? Did it say?"

"Yes." Jem nodded, proudly. "Someone walking his dog, last thing at night. It was the dog that found me."

"Dogs do that," I said. "They're very good at finding things. Rags once found a baby bird in the middle of the road, and know what? He didn't even *try* to eat it. Dad picked it up and put it in someone's garden."

"This dog barked," said Jem. "That's what made his owner come and look. If it hadn't been for him – " her eyes grew large, with wonderment – "if it hadn't been for him I might have *died*."

Me and Skye sat down next to her, on the top step.

"What kind of person," said Skye, "leaves a newborn baby outside in the middle of winter?"

"Someone desperate," I said.

"You mean, someone heartless!"

"Not necessarily. She could have been

young, like *really* young, like… fifteen, maybe? And she'd have been scared. In a panic! She wouldn't have known what she was doing. I once read somewhere," I said, "that having a baby can drive you a bit nuts. Just temporarily. It wears off," I assured Jem, who was starting to look worried. "I'm not saying your mum was mad, or anything."

"Just heartless," muttered Skye.

"Don't keep *saying* that!" Jem shoved at her. "Imagine how you'd feel if you had a baby when you were only fifteen and you couldn't tell your mum and dad cos they'd, like, disown you or something."

"Pardon me," said Skye, "but if I had a baby when I was only fifteen I think my mum and dad might notice."

"They don't always," I said. "I've heard about girls having babies and nobody even knowing they were pregnant. Sometimes they didn't even know it themselves."

"Excuse me?" said Skye.

"No, she's right, she's right!" said Jem. "I've heard that too."

"And it's a Catholic church," I said, "so that could mean she was Catholic. It's a sin," I said, "if you're Catholic."

The more I thought about it, the more I began to feel sorry for this unknown girl, whoever she might have been.

"It's a tragedy," I said.

"It could have been," agreed Jem. "If that dog hadn't found me."

"No, but for *her*."

Even Skye had to admit, as we crossed back over the main road and wandered for old times' sake along the Arcade, that it wouldn't be easy if you were only fifteen and your mum and dad weren't the sort of people you could talk to.

"On the other hand," I said, "it is kind of romantic… it's not everyone gets left on the steps of a church."

"It's not, is it?" said Jem, brightening. "I wish they'd kept the shawl, though."

"Maybe they did. Maybe if you asked your mum…"

But she wasn't ready for that. For the moment she seemed content just knowing something about her beginnings.

"My *real* beginnings," she said.

CHAPTER SIX

I thought when I arrived home that Mum would be eager to hear about the Arcade, and whether the children's playground was still there. I thought she'd be interested to know how Jem had got on, finding the very church, the very *steps*, where she had been abandoned.

"It was just, like, so extraordinary," I said. "Sitting there, right on the actual spot!"

"I'm sure it must have been," said Mum. "But

before you go any further I think I should warn you… your father is not in the best of moods. He is not at all pleased with you."

I said, "What? Why?" What had I done now?

"He's hopping mad," said Angel.

But I hadn't *done* anything! And then I noticed Rags: all along one side he was covered in something white. *Paint?*

Mum pointed silently up the stairs. I didn't want to look, but she seemed to expect it of me. Reluctantly, I swivelled my eyes in the direction of her pointing finger. Great clumps of dog fur were sticking out of Dad's paintwork. You could see where Rags had bumped and banged against it as he careered down the stairs.

"Furry skirting boards!" sniggered Tom.

Dad had appeared on the upstairs landing. "I am not amused," he said.

"No one ever is." Angel said it bitterly. "The

things she gets up to."

I said, "I didn't do it! It was Rags."

"Oh, *please*," said Angel.

"That's right, go blaming an innocent dog," said Dad.

It wouldn't have been so bad if he'd been a white dog. Unfortunately, he's grey. And he has this really long hair.

"Maybe it'd pull off—" I grabbed at a bunch and yanked. The hair came away, but so did some of the paintwork. Dad howled.

"Don't touch it! You'll only make matters worse."

I backed away, hastily.

"I have never known *anyone*," said Dad, "capable of creating such havoc."

"Well, I'm sorry," I said. "But how was I to know the door bell would ring?"

"Cos it's what door bells do," said Angel. "Specially," she added, "when you've got people coming."

"I didn't know they were going to arrive just at that moment! I was *brushing* him," I said. She had some nerve. "Not like you ever lift a finger to do him!"

"That's cos he's not my dog. I wanted a rabbit, remember? If I'd had a rabbit," said Angel, "I'd have brushed him every single day. You were the one that insisted on carting that great lumping thing home."

"Yes, you'd just have left him there to go mouldy!" We'd found him at the rescue centre. He'd looked so forlorn, all alone in his cage. "Poor little man!"

"Little?" shrieked Angel. "He's the size of a cart horse!"

"And he's ruined my paintwork," said Dad.

"Would you like me to re-do it?" I said.

"I don't think so," said Dad. "Thank you all the same."

"I could!"

"I'm sure you could. You'd no doubt paint

the stair carpet and the hall table and the front door mat while you were at it."

Why would I do that? Honestly! People have such strange ideas.

"I'm only trying to help," I said.

"What you don't seem to understand," hissed Angel, "is that nobody *wants* your help."

Well, she was wrong there, cos Jem did! For the first few days after our pilgrimage, she'd been happy just preening. Basking in her newfound glory. Abandoned! In a shawl! What could be more romantic? But once the immediate excitement started to wear off, she began to get worked up and wail that she had to find out more.

"I have to know who she was!"

Even Skye was prepared to admit that it was a mystery which needed to be solved.

"You might not like what you discover, but now that you've come this far I guess you have to go on."

The problem was, none of us had the least idea what to do next.

"We've got to do *something*," I said to Skye. Finding her birth mum was all Jem could talk about. All day, every day. First break, second break. On the way to school, on the way back home. *Why couldn't she keep me? What made her get rid of me? I've got to find out! I can't go through life not knowing!*

I tried to be patient, cos I could imagine what she must be feeling, but quite honestly it was getting to be just a little bit tiresome. Even, almost, a bit worrying.

"She's become just, like, totally obsessed!"

"You shouldn't ever have got her going in the first place," said Skye.

I said, "*Me?*"

"You were the one that suggested she start looking."

"Only cos she was in a state about her life being blighted."

"She's always in a state. You know what she's like! Give her a few days and she'd have forgotten all about it."

"Maybe," I said, hopefully, "she'll forget about this too?"

"Maybe," said Skye; but she didn't sound very optimistic. I wasn't very optimistic myself. I'd lost count of the number of things Jem had gone on about in the past, but this was different. This was really intense.

One Friday afternoon I went back with her after school. She said she had something she wanted to show me. Skye couldn't come as she had a music lesson, so it was just the two of us. I hadn't been round to Jem's for ages. Mrs McClusky was in the kitchen, standing all comfortable and roly-poly at the sink in a bright pink tracksuit. She was happily sloshing around with mounds of bubbles frothing and foaming across the draining board. Mum would go demented if I used that much washing-up liquid! Mrs McClusky obviously enjoyed having lots of bubbles.

"Hello, stranger!" She flapped a hand and water went spraying into the air. "I'm washing up from this morning." She laughed, happily. "And from last night! I bet your mum doesn't let dirty dishes mount up like this?"

It's true, she doesn't; but then my mum is at home all day. I know she's working, but Jem's mum has to go *out* and work. In the morning she's a school dinner lady (not at our school) and in the evening she cleans people's offices, so I could perfectly understand why it was she was doing last night's dishes at four o'clock the next day. It didn't seem to me at all unreasonable. Personally, if it were left to me, I would just dump everything in the sink and take stuff out when it's needed. I can't think all this washing up is good for the environment. But I felt sorry for poor Mrs McClusky, having to come home and do all this work and then go out cleaning offices.

"Shall I help?" I said.

"*No.*" Jem beckoned, impatiently. "I've got something I want you to see!"

"I'll just dry," I said. "And you can put away."

Jem screwed up her face as if in some kind of agony. I dried a cereal bowl and placed it carefully on the kitchen table. Ungraciously, Jem snatched it up, but before she could put it away her mobile had started ringing and she immediately plonked it back down again. I saw her glance at the caller ID.

"I've just got to go and take this," she said.

I gave up. She was away for so long that I had to start putting things away myself. If she'd taken the call in the kitchen she could have put things away at the same time, which means I wouldn't have tripped over my school bag and smashed a plate.

"Now look what you've done!" she said, reappearing at precisely the wrong moment.

She said it like it was my fault. Like if I hadn't insisted on helping, it wouldn't have happened.

Mrs McClusky just laughed and said not to worry. "It was probably cracked, anyway."

"I'll clear it up," I said.

"That's all right, just chuck it in the bin."

I really do love Jem's mum! There is no fuss and bother with her. Mum would have gone on and on about me leaving my school bag in the middle of the floor, and if the plate had been cracked to begin with she would have been bound to say that I had done it. I am responsible for everything!

Jem was tugging at me. "You coming, or not?"

"Yes, off you go!" Mrs McClusky waved us away. "You obviously have things to do."

"Who was on the phone?" I asked Jem.

"*That*," said Jem, "was *Liliana*. She's got another modelling job!"

I said, "Oh." I didn't know whether to be

sympathetic, like, "All right for some people," or whether to say something bracing on the lines of, "Don't worry, it probably won't last." In the end I didn't say anything, and neither did Jem. She just threw open the door of her bedroom and noisily banged it shut again behind us. I thought, uh-oh! Trouble ahead. I expected her to get going on her usual my-life-has-been-blighted routine, and was quite surprised when she didn't. It seemed that whatever it was she'd asked me round to see was more important.

I was curious. I bounced down on to her bed while Jem crawled on hands and knees across the floor, then lay flat on her side and groped with one hand under a chest of drawers. I watched with growing astonishment. What could be so secret that she had to keep it hidden from her mum? I know my mum has this truly annoying habit of prowling about my room when I'm not there, tidying things up and putting things away, but I don't think she would ever actually spy. Like if I kept a diary and wrote PRIVATE on the front, she wouldn't immediately sit down and have a read of it. I don't *think* she would. And if my mum wouldn't, then I didn't reckon Mrs McClusky would, either. Jem obviously had something she felt guilty about.

"Here." She handed me a cardboard folder that she'd slid out from under the chest. On the front it had a big red question mark.

"What is it?" I said.

"Have a look!" Jem seemed both excited and at the same time a bit anxious, like maybe I might not approve. Her face had turned a give-away pink.

I opened the folder. Inside was a drawing. A girl, quite young, with thick, black, glossy hair, big dark eyes and a creamy complexion. Rather like Jem herself. Underneath it said, *My birth mum?*

I stared at it for a while, wondering how to react.

"What do you think?" said Jem.

I swallowed. I didn't know what to think, quite honestly. "Did you copy it from somewhere?" I said.

"No! It came out of my head. It's what I think she might have looked like."

It was a good drawing. Art is one of Jem's best subjects. But I still didn't know what to think.

"Here." Jem reached across and pulled an envelope out of the folder. "Read this!"

On the envelope she'd printed the words, *Letter to my Daughter*. I took out a sheet of paper, covered in handwriting I didn't recognise. It wasn't Jem's round, bouncy hand.

I turned to her, puzzled. "Is this *really* from your birth mum?"

Jem giggled, a bit shamefaced. "No, it's something I made up. Read it!"

I really didn't want to; it felt like intruding. This was Jem's private dream world. Nothing to do with me! But she was waiting, eagerly watching, so I didn't have much choice.

"*My dearest darling daughter,*" I read, in the handwriting that wasn't Jem's.

"*I am walking into the churchyard with you in my arms. I will lie you down at the top of the steps where you will be sheltered from the wind. At least you have your nice warm shawl that I knitted for you. That is some comfort. I couldn't bear the thought of you being cold.*

"*Now I fear it is time for me to leave you. It breaks my heart to go but I am very scared and confused and do not know what else to do. There is no one I can speak to. My mum and dad are very harsh cruel people and I shudder to think what would happen if I told them about you. You are so precious to me!*

"*This is the moment I have been dreading. The moment when I must say goodbye. For ever!*

Goodbye, my dear little baby! I will give you one last kiss on your sweet soft cheek. I know you will not remember me but I will remember you until the end of my days. I will never stop thinking about you and wondering what has become of you. I love you so much, I pray with all my heart that you will find happiness in your life.

"*With all my love, Mum.*"

I finished reading and folded the letter back up. There was a long silence.

"Well?" Jem flung herself down next to me on the bed. "What d'you think? D'you think it's the sort of letter she might have written?"

Actually, to be honest, I thought it was kind of embarrassing. The sort of thing best kept hidden away and read only in strictest privacy. Preferably late at night, under the duvet, with a torch. But Jem had her eyes fixed on me, obviously waiting for me to say something. I didn't want to hurt her. She's my friend and I knew how important it was. So I said yes, I thought it sounded exactly the sort of letter her birth mum might have written. Jem's face glowed with pleasure.

"Mind you," I said, "I don't quite see how she'd have been able to write it the same time she was saying goodbye."

Jem crinkled her nose. "How d'you mean?"

"Well… that bit about *I am walking into the churchyard with you in my arms*. How'd she manage to walk and write at the same time?"

Jem obviously hadn't thought of that. The pinkness came surging back into her cheeks. So then I felt mean and wished I hadn't said anything.

"P'raps it was artistic licence," I said. "Like, she went home and sat down to write the letter and was kind of re-living things in her mind?"

"Mm." Jem nodded, slowly. "'Cept I imagined her writing it *before*. So's she could leave it with me, you know?"

"OK! So instead of *re*-living it she was *pre*-living it."

I thought that was pretty neat, and so did Jem. She liked that explanation. Her face went into a big happy beam.

"Of course –" she said it bravely – "if there *is* a letter it probably won't be anything like this one."

"You never know," I said. "It might be. Are you…" I waved at the folder. "Are you planning on adding anything else?"

"Like what? What sort of things d'you think I could add?" She leant forward, excitedly. "I thought of more photographs. Ones when she was younger? Like my age? And maybe she'd have left me a school report, or something, so I'd know what kind of things she was good at. See if they're the kind of things I'm good at. That'd be interesting, wouldn't it? Don't you think?"

I said, "Yes. Why not?" But I can't have sounded very convincing cos Jem suddenly dropped her gaze and began plucking at the duvet.

"I know it's only pretend," she muttered. "But it's all I've got!"

On the way home I called Skye on my mobile.

"You know we were talking about Jem being obsessed?" I said. "Well, it's getting worse!" I told her about the folder and the letter.

"Hm. Acting out her fantasies," said Skye.

"But I think she really believes them! She says it's only pretend, but then she says it's all she's got."

"I dunno what we can do."

"We've got to help her find her birth mum!"

But how, that was the problem?

CHAPTER SEVEN

Next day, which was Saturday, I found myself in the bathroom with Mum, explaining how it couldn't possibly have been me that had left the hot tap running cos last time I'd used it the water had come out boiling hot and I'd got burnt, so now I only used the cold.

"I wash in *cold water*," I said. "It's good for you! And it saves on electricity."

"Whereas leaving the tap running does anything but," said Mum.

"Well, exactly! That's why I wouldn't do it. Ooh, that must be the post!" Rags had started his postman bark at the front door. "I'll get it!"

Apart from the fact that I enjoy collecting letters off the front door mat, I was glad to get away before Mum could start falsely accusing me. I wasn't the one that wasted water! Even if I'd turned the hot tap on by mistake, which I just might have done, I'd have quickly turned it back off. I wouldn't want to get burnt again, would I?

I hurtled down the stairs to find Rags busily ripping and tearing at something. Fortunately it was the local paper, not the post, but I still yelled at him.

"Rags! Get off!"

I like the local paper, it has interesting headlines. Like last week it had been, *DOCTORS CURED MY SON'S FLAT HEAD.* This week it was, *RAT THE SIZE OF CAT IN WOMAN'S BACK GARDEN*, except I couldn't get to read about it cos of Rags having torn the front page to shreds.

"Stupid dog!" I said, but he only grinned, like it was some big joke. He never takes me seriously.

I sat at the foot of the stairs to read what was left. Mostly sport and cars. I'm not into either of them, so I chucked the pages at Rags, who immediately jumped on them and began his shredding act. Near the back of the paper there's a page called *YOUTH CULTURE*. That is more my sort of thing. Rags had torn it down the middle, so I fitted the pieces together – and had a bit of a shock. Cos there, staring up at me, was a girl who looked incredibly like the drawing Jem had done of her birth mum. There was a long interview with her, taking up half the page, under the heading *LOCAL GIRL MAKES GOOD*.

Her name was Mia Jelena, and it seemed she was some kind of a singer.

"Have you ever heard of her?" I asked Angel, who had just rudely shoved past me on her way down the stairs.

"Who?" She peered over my shoulder. "Mia Jelena? Of course I've heard of her! She's famous. Hey, give me that!"

She made a grab at the paper, but I whisked it out of her way.

"I got it first!"

"Looks like that dog got it first."

"He likes to read things," I said. "He's an intellectual. You can have it when I'm through."

"Well, just don't take all day!"

"I won't," I said. "I'm a very fast reader."

But by the time I came to the end of the article I'd forgotten all about Angel. My heart was pumping, furiously. The blood was pounding in my ears. I'd solved Jem's mystery!

It was all there, in front of me, *printed in the paper*. It couldn't be clearer! I forced myself to stay calm – a little bit calm – and started to read the article again, more slowly, this time, just to make sure. I wouldn't want to get Jem's hopes up for nothing.

LOCAL GIRL MAKES GOOD

It's only been a few months since singer Mia Jelena released her first attention-grabbing album, Gonna Get Going, *for Pineapple Records, but already she's being hailed as the new Queen of Soul. Now she's back with album no. 2,* There's Got to be Love, *and she's coming to the Daycroft Halls on 15ᵗʰ December as part of a nationwide tour to celebrate her success.*

I asked Mia how it felt, to be coming back to the town where she grew up and where, as she herself has admitted, life was not always easy. She agrees that it wasn't, but says that that is all behind her.

"I can look back now and remember the good times, not just the bad."

I ask her what the good times were, and she says, "Mainly school. I went to Hillcrest and I made lots of really great friends there, though I didn't always behave as well as I should. I used to get into lots of trouble for talking too much and not paying attention. I was a bit of a naughty girl in those days!"

And the bad times? She doesn't shy away from the question.

"The bad times," she says, "were being in a children's home and then with foster parents. We didn't really get on. I can see now that it was probably my fault as much as theirs, but we had absolutely nothing in common and it made for a very difficult few years."

"I believe you actually left home when you were only sixteen?"

"Yes, I did."

"That's a very young age to strike out on your own."

"I just felt like I had no alternative.

Something happened… I got into a bit of trouble. I knew I couldn't turn to my foster parents. I was desperate! I had to get away."

"Can I ask where you went?"

"I didn't really go anywhere, in the sense of heading for any particular place. To start off with, I just drifted, until in the end I found my way to London. Inevitable, really." She pulls a face. "Where else does a runaway go? We all think the streets there are paved with gold."

"But you survived."

"I think I had a certain toughness which made me grit my teeth and just get on with things. I scraped a living. I worked in clubs, I worked in shops… One thing I was determined not to do, and that was to give up and go crawling back home with my tail between my legs. Little did I think…" She laughs, a rich gurgle of amusement. "Little did I think that one day I'd be returning as a minor celeb!"

I say, "Not so minor," and she shrugs a shoulder.

I ask her if she had always wanted to be a singer. She says that she always made a lot of noise. "I don't know if you'd call it singing!" But then she stops, and thinks about it, and says that is not quite true.

"I did used to sing. All the time. Just not in the school choir, you know? I'm not sure I ever consciously thought about the future, but I guess I always knew I was destined for show business in one form or another. I used to get into a whole load of trouble with my foster parents for what they called showing off. Making myself obvious. They didn't approve. I remember my foster mother once complaining that I never stopped fizzing and bubbling. I guess I still don't. The difference is that now I get paid for it!"

Reflecting on her path to fame Mia says that the most important thing for her was that she never gave up.

"No matter what happened, I never lost sight

119

of my goal. I was at my lowest ebb when I ran away. I thought my life was over, but in fact it was just beginning. Sheer determination carried me through."

Omigod! I could hardly contain myself. I felt like rushing round to Jem's straight away, but remembered just in time that she wouldn't be there. They were all going off for the weekend to stay with her nan and granddad. They wouldn't be back, Jem had said, till late on Sunday evening. Oh bother, bother, bother, *bother*! I would burst if I didn't tell someone.

Maybe I could ring Skye? But that wouldn't be fair; Jem ought to be the one to hear first. I banged my fist down on the floor.

"Damnation and curses and picture skew oaths!"

"I think you'll find that word is pronounced *picturesque*," said Dad, coming out of the front room. "*Picture-esk.*"

Rather huffily I said, "Whatever."

"Very colourful language, coming from you!"

"It's instead of swearing," I said. "I didn't think you'd like it if I used swear words."

"I'd be shocked if you knew any."

"I know plenty!" I shouted, as he went past me up the stairs.

"Please," said Dad, "don't ruin my illusions. What's to swear about, anyway?"

"I've just discovered something totally earth-shattering and I can't tell anybody!"

"Why can't you? Is it a state secret?"

"No! It's cos Jem's gone away and she's the one that has to know first and I won't see her until Monday!"

"Well, just remember," said Dad, "patience is a virtue."

I have lots of virtues. I do! I really do. Not boasting, but I am very loyal to my friends and hardly ever lose my temper and am extremely tolerant of other people's annoying faults and failings. I just find it VERY DIFFICULT to be patient.

I went up to my room, accompanied by Rags, and read the article yet again, just to make absolutely certain I wasn't imagining things. But I wasn't! I sellotaped the torn edges, took a red felt tip pen out of my school bag and began underlining all the important parts.

Local girl... went to Hillcrest... left home when you were only sixteen... got into a bit of trouble... NEVER STOPPED FIZZING AND BUBBLING. I underlined that bit three times and put a row of exclamation marks at the side. I couldn't wait for Monday morning to arrive!

But then, guess what? Monday morning comes at last – and *Jem isn't there.* Not at our usual meeting place on the way to school. She's late. Again!

"I'm not waiting," said Skye.

"Just a few more minutes," I begged.

"*No.*" Skye set off without so much as a backward glance. I hovered a moment, then reluctantly went trailing after her.

"Did you see the local paper?" I said.

"No," said Skye. "Did you do your maths homework?"

I dismissed my maths homework with an airy flick of the hand. Last week I'd forgotten to do it and had been put in the dreaded Book with a black mark against my name. So what? Who cared? There were more important things to think about!

"I read this really interesting article," I said.

"About what?"

"About this singer? Mia Jelena?"

"Never heard of her."

"Angel has. She says she's famous. There's a picture of her… I've brought it in to show you. Well… show Jem, really. She's the one I've brought it for. And the article. You'll never believe what it says!"

"What?"

I sucked in my breath. "Can't tell you! I shouldn't even be talking about it. Not without Jem."

We both turned, and looked back the way we had come.

"Seems like you'll have to wait till break," said Skye.

"I've been waiting all weekend! I was going to call her, but they'd gone away. I nearly called you, only I thought p'raps it wouldn't be fair. You see, it's about her birth mum... I think I might have solved the mystery!"

Well, at least I had her attention. Skye stopped, and frowned. "How?"

"It's no good, I can't tell you! It's in the article."

"Just give me a hint."

"No, I can't." I shook my head. "But it's more

than coincidence. It's got to be!"

"What is?" said Skye. "*What* is more than coincidence?"

"What it says. I can't tell you!"

She nagged at me all the way to school, but I wouldn't say a word. Like I say, I am very loyal to my friends. Jem would never forgive me if I let Skye into the secret of my amazing discovery without her being there to share it.

I was just terrified in case Jem wasn't going to be in school at all that day, cos loyal though I am I wasn't sure how much longer I could last before my mouth went and opened of its own accord and everything came spilling out. It wasn't right that Skye kept poking and prying! She shouldn't have been tempting me like that.

When I hissed at her about it, under cover of Mrs Gently taking registration, she got all high and mighty and hissed back that I shouldn't ever have mentioned anything in the first place.

"If you'd just kept *quiet*—"

"I thought I could trust you!"

Fortunately, before a situation could develop, the door had opened a crack and Jem had come sidling in, hoping, no doubt, that Mrs Gently (who is a bit dozy) wouldn't have noticed her absence. She didn't! Quite extraordinary. I immediately scribbled a note and pushed Skye out of the way so I could shove it across the desk to Jem.

Sumthing 2 tell U at break!!!

Jem mouthed at me. "What?"

I couldn't mouth back at her as Skye had meanly sat up very stiff and straight and blocked my view. She was doing it on purpose! In a huff cos I hadn't let her into the secret.

The minute the bell rang for break we

headed for our private corner.

"She's been driving me mad," said Skye. "She's discovered something and she won't say what!"

"I told you," I said, "we had to wait for Jem."

"Well, so now she's here, so you can tell us!"

"Before I do—" Skye groaned, and rolled her eyes. "Before I *do*," I said, turning to Jem, "have you ever heard of Mia Jelena?"

"No," said Jem. "Who is she?"

"It's who she *might* be," I said. I folded the paper so that only the photograph could be seen. Jem gazed at it, wonderingly. "Do you recognise it?"

"N-no… I don't think so."

"It looks a bit like you," said Skye.

Hah! I knew I hadn't been imagining it.

"You don't think you could have seen it somewhere and that's what made you do that drawing?" I said. "That drawing of your birth mum?"

"No." Jem was very positive. "That came out of my head."

"Is she the singer?" said Skye, pointing at the photo.

"Yes. She's the Queen of Soul, and she's coming to the Daycroft Halls on 15th December. She's coming back to where she used to live… See?" I flashed the headline at them. "*LOCAL GIRL MAKES GOOD*. Shall I read it to you? I'll read it to you!"

I read it very slowly and clearly, pausing for effect at all the places where I'd underlined.

"Mainly school. *I went to Hillcrest—*"

"She came here?" said Jem.

"Yes! It's what she says… *I went to Hillcrest.* Listen! There's more."

I saw Jem's eyes widen as I read the bit about Mia leaving home when she was only sixteen. They widened even more as I got to *something happened… I got into a bit of trouble.* By the time I came to *never stopped fizzing and bubbling* they were practically sticking out on stalks.

"There!" I said, when I'd finished. "What d'you reckon?"

Skye opened her mouth. I rushed in hastily, before she could start being negative. "Don't try saying it's just coincidence!"

"I wasn't going to," said Skye. "I was going to say… "

"What?"

"I was going to say wow." She muttered it a bit shamefacedly.

Wow is *not* one of Skye's expressions. It showed she was impressed, not to say totally gobsmacked. Hah! I turned, triumphantly, to Jem.

"So what d'you think?" I poked at her. "Oi! What d'you think?"

Jem seemed to have gone into a trance. She had taken the page from me and was staring, open-mouthed, at the photo.

"That could be my mum," she said. Her eyes had gone the size of soup plates. "She could be my mum... and she's famous!"

CHAPTER EIGHT

"She does look like you," said Skye.

"That's what got me," I said. "I saw it *immediately*. That's why I thought maybe you'd copied your drawing from somewhere."

"I didn't," said Jem. " I just—" She blushed. "I just looked at a picture of me and made it older."

"Well," I said, "that practically proves it… it's just too much to be a coincidence!"

I looked at Skye, daring her to deny it. She

frowned, but didn't actually say anything. Jem was eagerly rereading the article, in search of more clues. She pounced, gleefully.

"*I get into trouble for talking too much and not paying attention!*"

She did; all the time.

"And *I* don't have anything in common with my mum and dad! And I'm always showing off!"

"You fizz and pop," I said.

"I've always fizzed and popped! D'you remember, at primary school—"

"Yes, yes," said Skye. "We all remember at primary school."

"You used to call me Fizzy Pop!"

"We did," said Skye, kindly. "But it still doesn't actually *prove* anything."

I knew she'd have to start being negative. "What more proof do you want?" I said.

"Well, for a start," said Skye, "we don't know how old Mia is. If she's only, like, twenty, then that'd obviously make her too young."

I checked, hurriedly, on my fingers. Jem was eleven, and twenty minus eleven was… nine. Oops! Skye was right. Far too young.

"Whereas," said Skye, who likes to use these sort of words, "if she was *thirty*—"

"She's not thirty!"

"You don't *know*."

We all gazed at the photo, trying to decide how old Mia might be.

"Photos can be airbrushed," said Skye. "She could be any age. It's no good just guessing, we have to be sure."

"But how?" quavered Jem.

"Look her up on the Internet. If she's famous, like Angel says, there's bound to be a website or something." It was at that point, most annoyingly, that the bell rang for the end of break. Jem let out a howl.

"I need to know *now*!"

"Leave it to me," said Skye. "I'll find out. I'll tell Mrs Holliday I've got to check something urgently. She'll let me."

Mrs Holliday is our librarian. She wouldn't have let me or Jem go on the computer when we were supposed to be in class, but Skye is one of her favourites. Skye is lots of teachers' favourite. I don't hold it against her; it is just the way she is.

"At least," I pointed out to Jem, "it shows she's taking things seriously at last."

If she was late for registration she'd run the risk of being put in the Book. Her worst nightmare! I mentioned this to Jem, who said, "Yes, I suppose," but in a vague sort of way. She kept shooting these worried glances at the door. I guessed she was scared in case Skye came back and reported that Mia had been airbrushed and was in fact quite ancient.

Skye slid into class just as registration had started. Mr Keys said, "You can think yourself lucky, Skye Samuels, that you're in the second half of the alphabet." He wouldn't have said that to me! Not, of course, that I am in the second half of the alphabet, but that is not the point. The point is, he would have torn me to shreds. Still, I guess that is life. You just have to accept it.

Skye slipped into her place between me and Jem. Slowly and deliberately, she held out her hand, palm upwards, on the desk. She was trying to show us something! I craned forward to look. On it, in ball point pen, she had written: 27. I did more hasty calculations on my fingers. Twenty-seven minus eleven was … sixteen. Yay! It worked out exactly. Jem's face was now bright pink with excitement. She spent the rest of the morning taking sly peeks at Mia's photograph. If she wasn't careful, I thought, she would have it confiscated. Some of our teachers are unbelievably strict.

At lunch time, we crammed down our food as fast as we could and headed off to our private den.

"She's my mum," exulted Jem. "I know she is! It's just this feeling I have."

"Me too," I said.

We both turned, automatically, to Skye.

"Don't you agree?" said Jem. "Don't you think she's my mum?"

"I guess she might be," said Skye.

"So should I get in touch with her or not?"

"I'm not sure." For once in her life, Skye sounded doubtful. "I don't quite see how we can."

"Maybe," I said, "if we got tickets for her show?"

"You must be joking," said Skye. "It'll be well sold out by now."

"And where would we get the money?" Jem bleated it, pathetically. "My mum was going to take me to the Ice Dance but the tickets cost, like, a *fortune.*"

I am not one to give in. I find it really

irritating when all people can do is raise objections. Specially when you are trying to help them!

"Just cos we can't get tickets," I said, "doesn't stop us going there. We could wait at the stage door."

Skye gave a hollow laugh. "At eleven thirty at night?"

Wild thoughts of creeping out of the house while Mum and Dad were in bed, or watching television, flashed through my brain; but even I could see that that might be fraught (as they say) with difficulties.

"We've got to do *something*," pleaded Jem.

"We'll have a think. We will all rack our brains," said Skye.

I racked like crazy the whole afternoon. I thought, *we could write a letter*. Well, Jem could write a letter. She could leave it at the box office. I began composing it in my head.

Dear Ms Jelena,

I am a great fan of your music. (It was only diplomatic to say that.) *I wish I could have come to your concert tonight, but I could not get tickets. My mum could not afford them.* (Hopefully that would make Mia feel sorry for Jem.)

When I say "my mum" what I mean is my mum that adopted me. I have been trying to trace my birth mother, and when I read about you in the local paper—

Which was as far as I could get. No matter how many times I wrote and rewrote in my head, I always became stuck at the same place. How do you ask someone you have never met if they are your real mum who abandoned you when you were just a tiny baby?

By afternoon break I was beginning to feel slightly demented. I think Jem was too. Her face was all scrunched up with the effort of brain-racking, and her hair was a mad mess of tangles. Skye was the only one looking calm.

"What we ought to do," she said, "is see if we can find her in one of the school photos. All those great long ones they've got in the main corridor? They go back decades. She must be in one of them. I know it won't actually *tell* us anything, but the more we discover the better."

"*Yes!*" Jem was practically bouncing on the spot. She wanted to rush off and start looking right there and then, but we are not allowed in school during break. I have no idea why; it is just another of their rules. Maybe the teachers like to get up to things while we are not there, though it is hard to think what.

"After school," said Skye. "We'll do it after school."

Fortunately, from my point of view, the last lesson of the afternoon was PE. I like PE! Today it was hockey and I especially like hockey.

I think it is hugely satisfying to tear up and down the field whacking at the ball and cracking your hockey stick against other people's sticks. For a while it meant that I was able to give my brain a well-deserved rest. Skye thinks hockey is barbaric and Jem once got whacked on the ankle and now tends to turn and run whenever she sees the ball coming towards her.

"You are such a nutter," grumbled Skye, as I walloped after her and Jem on our way back to the changing room.

"I bet Mia didn't like hockey," said Jem. "If she did, I'd have inherited it. Like your mum was probably a nutter like you."

"My mum was in the First Eleven," I said. "She had her name in the school magazine."

"Mia might have had her name in the magazine! Not for hockey. For singing, probably. I bet she did! I bet—"

"This is all irrelevant," said Skye. "I thought

we were going to go and look at photos?"

In the front hall and all along the main corridor are photographs going right back to when the school first opened. Skye led the way to the most recent ones.

"They're only taken once every five years so we'll have to look from *here* –" she tapped a finger – "to *here*. You start with that one," she told Jem, "and you –" she gave me a little push – "start with this one."

Skye can be incredibly bossy at times, but as she is good at organising and usually talks sense (when she is not being negative) I mostly just put up with it. I didn't mind which photograph she told me to look at. As it happens, it was one I am familiar with.

"Look," I said. "That's my auntie."

"Ooh! Where?" Skye craned to see.

"There, in the top row. Year 11."

"I didn't know your auntie came here."

"My mum did too."

"I knew about your mum."

"She's just had a baby," I said.

"Your mum?"

"My auntie."

"Oh!" Skye laughed. "For a minute I thought you meant your mum!"

Jem's voice hissed accusingly at us: "I thought we were supposed to be looking for *my* mum?"

"Yes, yes, we are! I'll find her," I said. "She's got to be here."

Nobody ever escapes school photographs. Not unless they have a really good excuse, like being abducted by aliens. It was Skye, in the end, who discovered Mia, sitting cross-legged and beaming in the front row. She was in the same photograph as Auntie Cath. Jem squealed, excitedly.

"It's her! It's my mum!"

"*Maybe* your mum."

"No, it is! It's got be. It all fits!"

We stood, looking at the picture of Mia when she was young. There was definitely a resemblance.

"Imagine her being here at the same time as your auntie," marvelled Skye. "Now *that's* a coincidence."

Jem spun round, her eyes shining. "Your auntie might have known her! She might be able to tell us something. Could we go and see her?"

"I suppose we could say we wanted to see the baby," I said. We'd obviously need an excuse of some sort. If I told Mum we were trying to find out as much as we could about somebody who might be Jem's birth mum she'd only start on at me again about my habit of interfering.

"When can we go?" said Jem. "Could we go now?"

"I'll have to check with Mum first."

"See if we can go tomorrow. We could go in lunch break!"

"Excuse me," said Skye. "We're not allowed out in lunch break."

"Who's going to find out?" Jem twirled, defiantly. "People do it all the time."

"It'd be easy enough," I said. "My auntie only lives ten minutes away."

"In that case," said Skye, "we can go after school." She was very firm about it. She'd already done her bit, begging favours from Mrs Holliday and almost being late for registration. She'd got away with it once, but she wasn't risking it a second time. "Ask your mum if we can go tomorrow. OK?"

I said OK and cornered Mum as soon as I got home. She was in the kitchen, mixing stuff in a bowl.

"Oh," I said, "you're cooking! Would you like me to help?"

"I'd rather you didn't," said Mum. "These are for our dinner tonight."

I was silent, wondering what she meant. Would she have wanted me to help if they *hadn't* been for our dinner? I didn't get it!

"Well, all right," I said. "If you don't want me to, I won't. But children are supposed to help their parents. By the way—" I scooped up a bit of glop that had splodged over the side of the mixing bowl. "Yummy! Would it be OK if I took Jem and Skye to see the new baby?"

"I don't see why not. You'd have to give Auntie Cath a ring, though, to check when it's convenient."

"I'll go and ring her right now," I said.

Auntie Cath wasn't there, so I left a message on her voicemail and went back to the kitchen, where I found Mum frantically splashing dollops of splodge on to a baking tray.

"Oh, Frankie," she said, "you can be of some

help, after all. My four thirty's just arrived, so if you could finish off here for me… all you need do is just make these into nice firm shapes, brush a bit of egg over them and put them in the oven. Do you think you could manage that?"

"No problem," I said.

"And don't let that dog have the mixing bowl, he'll put his teeth through it."

I promised that I wouldn't let Rags anywhere near the mixing bowl.

"It's all right," I said. "You can trust me."

Mum went off and I began carefully moulding all the little rissoles into neat shapes. I made some of them square, and some I made round, and some I made long and sausage-like. Mum is a good cook, I think, but she doesn't always have much imagination. After I'd finished with the shaping I wiped out the mixing bowl with my finger and gave the finger to Rags to lick, then put the bowl in the sink, out of his reach. I felt proud of myself for remembering. *Don't let Rags near the mixing bowl!* And I hadn't. Mum would be pleased with me.

I'd just about finished brushing egg yolk over my assortment of shapes when my mobile rang. Rags immediately started barking; he always barks when the phone rings. He seems to think it is some kind of intruder. It was Auntie Cath, calling me back. I took the phone into the garden.

"How's Henry?" I said.

"He's fine," said Auntie Cath. "He's just thrown up all over me!"

Some people might think *yuck* on hearing that a baby has thrown up over someone, but it doesn't strike me that way. It's like when Rags throws up. He is only a dog: a baby is only a baby. They don't know any better.

I asked Auntie Cath if I could come round with Jem and Skye after school next day, "cos they really, really want to see Henry." Auntie Cath is so sweet! She said she would love it if we went round.

I rang Jem to tell her, and we had a bit of a chat about Mia, with Jem wanting to know whether I really thought she could be her birth mum, and whether I really thought they looked alike.

"You're not just *saying* it?"

I assured her that I wasn't. Jem would have liked to carry on talking, but I told her I had to go.

"I just remembered… I'm supposed to be putting something in the oven!"

I went back to the kitchen and found to my surprise that the rissoles had disappeared. So had the baking tray. Mum must have come back and seen them there and put them in the oven herself. Well, that was all right. I'd made them into interesting shapes and brushed them with egg yolk, and Rags hadn't got the mixing bowl. Mum could hardly complain!

I went upstairs, feeling virtuous, to make a start on my homework. Some time later I heard the door of the front room open and Mum call out.

"Frankie? Angel? Anyone there? Tom? Oh, Angel! Just go and take the rissoles out of the oven, would you?"

"I'll do it!" I yelled. They were my rissoles. I'd made them into shapes! I wasn't having Angel take the credit.

I raced into the kitchen to find that she had got there first.

"Where have they gone?" she said. She'd opened the door of the oven and was peering inside. "They're not here!"

"They've got to be," I said.

"Well, they're not! And what's *that*?" She sprang back, with a shriek. "*That!* Down there!"

I followed the direction of her quivering finger. Dog sick. Yuck! A great big gooey pile of it.

"Where are the rissoles?" said Angel.

We both turned to look at Rags, wagging guiltily in the doorway.

"He must have taken them out of the oven!"

"What, you think he's some kind of canine genius? You think he's learnt how to open the door?"

"Maybe it… came open."

"You mean, maybe you didn't close it properly!"

"No! I didn't do it. It wasn't me!"

"So who put them in there?"

I said, "Mum!"

Well, I thought she had. Suddenly, I was beginning to have doubts.

"Where's the tray?" said Angel. "He can't have eaten the tray!"

We found the tray under the fridge. Two of

the rissoles were still there; a square one, and
a sausage-shaped one.

It was a nasty moment.

CHAPTER NINE

Everyone seemed to think it was my fault Rags had eaten the rissoles.

"What I can't understand," said Skye, as we went off after school the next day to visit Auntie Cath, "is why you were stupid enough to leave him alone with them in the first place. You know he eats things!"

"He ate those eggs that time," said Jem.

I shouldn't ever have told her about the eggs. A dozen of them, all smashed.

"He licked them off the floor," I said.

"Yes, but only after he'd knocked them there."

"Well, *that* wasn't my fault!"

Skye was still wittering on. "I can't understand why you had to go into the garden, anyway, just to answer the phone."

"He was barking," I said. "I couldn't hear."

"So why not put *him* in the garden?"

"Cos I didn't think!" My voice came out in a bit of a bellow. I will put up with A LOT, but Skye was really starting to get on my nerves. "If you want to know," I said, "I was too busy arranging for us to go and see the baby. I was thinking about Jem!"

"We're not *just* going to see the baby, though. Are we?" Jem looked at me, anxiously. "We are going to ask about Mia?"

"Yes, but we've got to see the baby first. He's very sweet," I said. "He's really cuddly. I wouldn't mind having a baby like him. I reckon

I'm going to have lots and lots of babies! Probably about... ooh, I don't know! Ten, maybe?"

"That would just be, like, totally gross," said Skye.

"Well, all right then! Five."

"That would still be gross. There's not going to be enough food to feed people as it is," said Skye. "Not when we have global warming."

She did have a point. "OK," I said, "I'll just have two. I suppose I'm allowed to have two? 'Specially if people like you aren't going to have any at all."

"I never said I wasn't going to have any at all! I j—"

"I wish you'd stop talking about babies and work out what we're going to say to your auntie," wailed Jem.

I told her that I knew what we were going to say. "We're going to say we're interested in

Mia cos of her being a celeb and being at our school."

"And you'd better let me and Frankie do the talking," said Skye. "We all know what'll happen if you start up."

She meant that Jem would give the game away. We'd already decided that we couldn't tell Auntie Cath the real reason we were interested in Mia. Apart from anything else she might go and mention it to Mum and then I'd be in *big* trouble. Even bigger than the trouble I was already in for letting Rags eat the rissoles. Mum had been pretty unpleasant about that.

We didn't spend very long looking at the baby. We all had a cuddle and made lots of cooey-gurgly noises, but Skye really isn't into babies, whatever she says, and Jem was practically dancing a jig with impatience. In fact she was jigging about so much that Auntie Cath asked her if she needed the loo.

Really embarrassing! Well, it was for Jem. I just giggled.

We all went to sit in the kitchen and drink Coke and eat cookies. Jem kicked at me under the table: I kicked her back. She mouthed at me, furiously. OK, OK! Time to ask the big question.

"When you were at school," I said to Auntie Cath, "did you ever know Mia Jelena?"

"Oh, Mia!" Auntie Cath laughed. We all held our breath. "Yes, I think everyone at school knew her. She was always a bit of a – well! A bit of a tearaway. Had quite a reputation. I remember when I was in Year 12 and we sometimes had to do cloakroom duty – do you still have that? Year 12s acting like a sort of police force?"

We nodded, solemnly.

"Well, I just dreaded it if Mia was around. She used to play us up something rotten! Not that she was malicious, or anything. Just totally hyper. Couldn't keep still, couldn't keep quiet—"

"Always fizzing and bubbling," said Jem.

Me and Skye glared at her across the table.

"Yes! That's exactly the way to describe it. It was like she might go pop at any minute. One of my friends had a sister in the same class? She used to hang out with Mia. I remember her mum was always worried in case Mia led her into trouble."

"What sort of trouble?" Jem said it eagerly. "Boys?"

"She certainly liked the boys."

"Did she ev—"

I interrupted, hastily. "We're only asking," I said, "cos of her being at Hillcrest and being so famous."

"It's like she's a sort of role model," said Skye.

"She's done really well for herself, hasn't she?" nodded Auntie Cath.

"Did you ever think she would?" said Jem.

"I suppose, looking back... I'm not totally surprised. She was the sort of person whose life could have gone either way. Up or down. Nothing in between. She was never going to just muddle along in the middle like the rest of us. She was a real live wire."

"It said in this article," said Skye, "she ran away from home when she was only sixteen?"

"Yes, I saw that. In the local paper, wasn't it? I vaguely remember it happening. I'd left school by then, but I remember my friend Anna saying how the police had gone round to talk to her sister—"

Jem leant forward. "The one that hung out with Mia?"

"Yes. They wanted to know if she had any idea where she might have gone."

"Did she?"

"She said not. I'm not sure they altogether believed her."

"You don't think she was having a baby, do you?"

O-mi-god. Would nothing shut her up? I tried frantically to think of something to say, but nothing came.

"I mean," mumbled Jem, "it's just an idea."

"She can't help it." Skye turned apologetically to Auntie Cath. "She has this thing about babies."

"She's been nagging at us for days," I said. *"When can I see your auntie's new baby?"*

Jem's face was growing slowly crimson.

"She actually told us," said Skye, "she wants to have *ten.*"

"I did not!" Jem's voice was an indignant squawk. "That was Frankie!"

I said, *"Me?"*

"You know it was!" spluttered Jem.

"Whoever it was," said Auntie Cath, "I wouldn't advise it. One is enough to scramble your brain. Ten would just about turn it to mush!"

"Besides being just, like, totally *irresponsible*," I said.

For a minute, I thought Jem was going to burst a blood vessel. But it was her own fault! We'd *told* her to leave all the talking to me and Skye. She hunched herself up so that she was facing Auntie Cath. All we could see was her back, still quivering with rage.

"In the article she said that something happened."

"Yes, that's right. She did, didn't she?"

"So I was just trying to imagine what it could be," said Jem.

"Well, it was certainly one of the rumours, that she'd got herself pregnant. But there were so many rumours! She'd had a row with her foster parents, she'd gone off with her boyfriend, she'd met someone on the internet. If she *had* got herself pregnant, I doubt she'd have told her foster parents. Apparently they were very strict."

Jem flashed a triumphant glance at me and Skye. "Told you so!" she said, as we walked back home afterwards.

"Told us *what*, exactly?" said Skye.

"That I was the reason she left home! And you heard what your auntie said… about her being a live wire? I'm a live wire!" said Jem. "I'm an up and down sort of person. I bubble and fizz!"

It was true; we couldn't deny it.

"But if she left home cos she was having a baby—" I said.

"You mean, having *me*," said Jem.

"Well… maybe."

"What d'you mean, *maybe*?" Jem practically screamed it at me. Since speaking to Auntie Cath, she'd got herself all worked up. *Very* fizzy and bubbly. "How much more proof do you need? She *said*. She *told* us. Sh—"

"Look, just shut up for a minute and let Frankie talk," said Skye.

I was quite flattered when she said that; it's not very often anyone invites me to talk. Jem, needless to say, went off into a sulk.

"All I was wondering," I said, "was where did she go?"

"I thought London," said Skye.

"But she left Jem – I mean, the baby – whoever it was, she left it *here*. Why go all the way to London and then come back just to leave a baby in the churchyard?"

Jem made a loud, impatient, trumpeting noise. "She didn't come back! She wasn't *there*."

"But she said—"

"*In the end* I found my way to London." Jem obviously knew the article by heart. "Obviously she didn't go there till she'd had me. I reckon what happened, she covered things up as long as she could, like with baggy sweaters and stuff, cos you can do that," said Jem. "I've heard of people doing that! They suddenly have babies and nobody even knew they were pregnant."

"Yes, you said that before," said Skye.

"Well, I'm just telling you… that's what obviously happened. Course, someone must have helped her. A friend, or someone. Maybe the one the police spoke to. Your auntie's friend's sister, who said she didn't know anything. That's cos she'd have been sworn to s— Oh!" Jem suddenly clapped a hand to her mouth. "We should have asked her! Your auntie! We should have asked her where she was."

"What, her friend's sister?"

"Don't you see?" Jem flung out her arms. "She could be the one who helped her! Why didn't you ask?"

My mouth opened and shut like a goldfish. I glanced at Skye, to see if she had the answer, but it seemed she was just as clueless as I was. Why *hadn't* we asked? It was obvious, now I came to think of it. Mia couldn't have managed by herself; she'd have needed a friend.

"I *knew* I shouldn't have left things to you!" cried Jem. "We'll have to go back."

"No, we can't," said Skye. "I promised Mum I'd be home."

"So me and Frankie'll go back."

I somehow didn't fancy that. The last thing I wanted was to be a nuisance. "Maybe I could ring her," I said.

"*Now! Ring her now!*"

So that was what I did, standing in the middle of the street, calling Auntie Cath to ask if she knew where we could find her friend's sister. Auntie Cath seemed a bit surprised.

"Why would you want to know that?"

Lamely, I mumbled that I was researching a project for school.

"Sounds to me," said Auntie Cath, "like you're sticking your nose in where it doesn't belong! All this about Mia running away from home to have a baby… Even if she did – and it's a big if – it doesn't give you the right to go poking about in her private life."

I protested that I wasn't, but of course I was, so I expect it didn't quite ring true.

"In any case, you're out of luck," said Auntie Cath. "I lost touch with my friend Anna years ago, I have absolutely no idea where she's living. Or where her sister is. And I'm afraid I wouldn't tell you, even if I had. If you want to do research, I'm sure there's plenty of stuff you can get off the internet."

I muttered, "OK. Sorry."

"That's OK, I'm not having a go at you. I think perhaps you just got a bit overenthusiastic."

"You don't have to tell Mum," I said, "do you?"

"No, don't worry, I won't tell your mum!"

That was a relief. I didn't want Mum jumping

to conclusions and reading me one of her lectures. *How many times have I told you, Frankie, not to interfere?*

Jem was disgruntled. She said, "I bet she does know, really!"

"I'm not asking her again," I said.

"If you'd asked her while we were there she might have said!"

"If you hadn't kept talking all the time when we'd already told you not to," said Skye, "we might have had a chance. Now she's all suspicious and thinks we're prying."

"It was you that made her suspicious," said Jem. "Going on about me wanting ten babies!"

We were bickering now; all accusing one another.

"I blame you," said Skye as we parted company, Jem going off down Addersley Drive and me and Skye continuing straight on.

"Why me?" I said. "Why do I always get the blame for everything?"

"You were the one that gave her the idea. It hadn't ever occurred to her to go looking for her birth mum till you went and suggested it."

"Huh!" I brooded for a while, wondering whether to pursue the matter or just let it drop. I decided to let it drop. I am used to people saying things are my fault; it's nothing new. "Do you reckon Mia really could be her mum?" I said.

Skye thought about it. "It all fits. I just don't see how she's ever going to be able to prove it."

I sighed. I didn't either. We seemed to have explored every possibility. But now she had come this far, she couldn't just stop.

It was what Jem herself said next morning, as we met up for school. "I can't just *stop*!"

"No, you can't," I said. "There's got to be other things we can do."

I glared at Skye, daring her to be negative, but she nodded in a brisk and businesslike way and said, "We'll make a list." Skye is always making lists. She makes lists of everything. Things to Do, Things to Remember, Things to Look Up, Things to Think About. "We'll do it at break," she said. She looked warningly at me and Jem. "Not during lessons!"

At break we were heading to our usual spot when this big bossy girl from our class, Daisy Hooper, came bounding up.

"Why are you lot always going off on your own?"

"Wouldn't you like to know?" I said.

"Well, I would," said Daisy. "What are you up to?"

"We're a secret society," I said.

"What kind of secret society?"

"Not the kind that'd let you join!"

Daisy sniffed. "Wouldn't want to."

"Then why ask?"

"Cos people shouldn't have secret societies! It's anti-social."

"Not that it's any business of yours," said Skye, "but since you're obviously dying of nosiness I don't mind letting you in on it."

What?

Jem gave a little screech. "Don't tell her!"

"She's got to, now," said Daisy.

"We're conducting very important research," said Skye. "It's what's known as *an ongoing investigation.*"

Ooh! Cool.

"What's that mean?" said Daisy.

"Means it's nothing to do with you," I said.

She is such a busybody! Always poking her nose in.

"Right," said Skye, as Daisy went flouncing off. "Let's get on with it and do the list." She took out a pen, and her rough book. "THINGS TO TRY." She stood, pen poised. "OK! Who's got any suggestions?"

It turned out that nobody had. Skye tutted, impatiently.

"You've had the whole morning to think of something!"

"So have you," said Jem.

"Yes, but she's *your* birth mum. And *she* –" she pointed her pen at me – "was the one that started it all!"

I said, "You were the one that said make a list."

"I didn't expect to have to do it by myself!"

We were bickering again. We never bicker!

"OK," said Skye. "Calm down. *Think.*"

So we thought. This is what we came up with:

THINGS TO TRY:
1. Ask Mum
2. Ask Mia
3. Ask a government department

It wasn't much of a list, but it was all we could think of.

"Might as well start at the beginning," said Skye. "Ask your mum. That's the easiest."

"No." Jem shook her head, very fiercely. "I can't!"

Asking her mum had been my contribution, so naturally I felt the need to defend it. I pointed out that it was the one thing she could do immediately, and maybe put herself out of her misery. But Jem just said, "I can't." She then added that Liliana had been round again, with the latest pictures from her photo shoot. I took this to mean that Jem was having another surge of bitterness and resentment towards poor Mrs McClusky.

"I reckon that Liliana's just winding you up," said Skye.

Jem scowled. "She doesn't have to wind me up, I'm already wound up. I keep thinking how that could be me, going to photo shoots!"

"Well, all right, we can't force you," said Skye. "But I don't see how you think you're going to ask Mia."

"I'll write to her," said Jem. Asking Mia had been her suggestion. "I'll write and ask her!"

"I already tried that," I said. "I wrote one in my head. It doesn't work."

"Maybe if we all sat down together," pleaded Jem.

"You can't just write to celebs out of the blue, asking them if they're your mum," objected Skye. "I think we ought to try a government department. After all, that's what they're for. To help people."

We looked at her, doubtfully.

"It's a democracy!" cried Skye. "It's our right! We'll Google it," she said, as we went back into school. "*How to find your birth mother*. It's just a question of knowing where to look."

Skye has this touching faith in computers; she reckons you can ask them pretty well anything and they will come up with an answer. She promised that we would go to the library and do it at lunch time, but guess what? All the computers were in use; we couldn't get anywhere near them.

"This is just *so* frustrating," moaned Jem.

She was so busy being frustrated, swinging her bag and bashing at things, that she almost missed the squawks of triumph as Daisy Hooper and her mob came thundering up the steps from the main corridor.

"So much for you and your silly secret society," crowed Daisy. "*We* just heard that Mia Jelena's going to be special guest at Speech Day!"

"What?" Jem spun round.

"You heard," said Daisy. "But we heard first!"

Well! You would have thought such a piece of news would send Jem into instant overdrive. I waited for her to start fizzing and popping, but she fell strangely silent and stayed that way all afternoon. She didn't even respond when I elbowed Skye to one side and passed her a note. Something was going on!

  She waited till school finished, till we were almost home, before she broke it to us: "I've decided what I'm going to do!"

CHAPTER TEN

Needless to say, we were both desperate to know what she was planning.

"You're going to speak to her!"

"Nope."

"You're going to give her a letter?"

"Nope."

"You're going to… " We stopped. What else *could* she be going to do?

Whatever it was, Jem wasn't saying. She'd gone all bright-eyed and fizzing. But she still wouldn't tell!

"What is she up to?" I said, as Jem went racing off. Skye shook her head.

"Just hope she knows what she's doing."

I felt sure, by next day, she would be so bursting that she would *have* to tell us. We nagged at her and pleaded, but all she kept saying was, "You'll have to wait and see!"

"Well, but if you're not going to go and speak to her," said Skye, "and if you're not giving her a letter…" She paused, hopefully.

"You're sending her a text!"

"How could I?" said Jem. "I don't know her number."

"Is it something you're going to do on Speech Day?"

"Not telling!"

"If it is," said Skye, "you'd better make sure it's not something that's going to get you into trouble."

"Ooh, no, I might get put in the Book!" Jem

gave a little squeal of mock terror and clapped her hands to her face.

"Mrs Stanhope'd get really mad if you made a scene in front of all the local dignitaries."

Mrs Stanhope is our head teacher. She is very tall and elegant and rather stern.

I said, "*Are* you going to make a scene?"

I had this vision of Jem marching into the hall waving a home-made banner, or even worse, suddenly jumping up and shouting, "That's my mum!" It is the sort of thing she would be capable of. But she just said again that we would have to wait and see.

It wasn't like Jem; she is usually hopeless at keeping secrets. They just come bursting out of her! Skye said later that it was worrying.

"I don't want to get in trouble. Everyone knows we're her friends. They'll think we egged her on!"

"I'm not egging her on," I said.

"I didn't say you were! I said that's what

people would *think*. Anyway, it was you, at the beginning."

We were back to that. It was all my fault. As usual. Blame Frankie!

"There is such a thing as free will," I said.

"Yes, like there's egging people on and putting ideas in their head. Oh, this is going to be disastrous!" cried Skye. "I can feel it in my bones!

Speech Day was on Friday evening, in the main hall. It was a big event. Everybody's parents came, as well as the local dignitaries. I'd gone last year, with Mum and Dad, to watch Angel being given second prize for "All-round performance". Hah! What a joke. She wouldn't get one this year. Mum said since she'd discovered boys her school work had gone right off. Boys were all she ever thought about. How sad is that?

"At least I did *get* a prize," she said.

"Not when you were in Year 7."

"I did so! I got 'Highly Commended'. What have you got?"

I hadn't got anything, as she very well knew. But Jem had been chosen to read out her essay! That was better than any old measly prize.

"She's going to read it out in front of all the dignitaries!"

"Big deal," said Angel. "It's only the Mayor!"

"And Mia. She's a *celeb*."

"Yeah, like she'll be really impressed."

It was at this point that Mum intervened to say she really wished we'd stop trying to score points off each other. "It's become extremely tiresome."

"But Mum, it *is* a big deal," I said. "Only two people out of the whole school get to read out their essays."

"I agree," said Mum. "It's quite an achievement. What is Jem's essay about?"

"It's called 'Beginnings'," I said. "We all had

to do one. Including *her*." I pulled a face at Angel, who stuck out her tongue. Talk about infantile! You would never think she was in Year 10. "Jem wrote this lovely stuff about her mum and dad. Saying how they were her *real* mum and dad, and being adopted made her feel special? Miss Rolfe said it was heart-warming."

"It sounds it," said Mum. "I hope her mum and dad are going to be there to hear it?"

I knew that they were, cos Mrs McClusky had told me, just the other day, when I'd been round at Jem's. She'd been quite giggly and excited.

"I don't know what she's written, she won't tell us, she says it's a secret. We're totally in the dark!"

I assured her that there was no need to worry. "You'll really like it," I smiled at Mrs McClusky. "You'll be ever so proud!"

All the rest of the week Jem continued, in a

quiet sort of way, to fizz and bubble. You could see she was just dying to open her mouth and let it all spill out, but somehow she managed to resist. The nearest she came was a series of high-pitched squeaks, like a bat, before immediately clamping a hand to her mouth and spluttering, "No! I can't tell you!"

"You're really going to do it?" said Skye, as we walked home after school on Friday.

"I've got to!" For just a moment there seemed to be a slight note of doubt in Jem's voice. Skye pounced, immediately.

"Do you really think you ought to?"

Jem sucked in her lower lip and started nibbling at it. "Got to," she muttered.

"You haven't *got* to. Whatever it is—"

"I've got to!"

Now she wasn't just nibbling, she was actually *chewing*. Ouch! Painful.

"Leave her alone," I said to Skye.

"I don't want her doing anything stupid! You

know what she's like."

"It's her business," I said. "Nothing to do with us."

"Oh!" Skye reared up in pretend amazement. "Look who's talking!"

"We shouldn't interfere," I said. I felt good, saying that. Mum would approve! "If you really think it's right," I told Jem, "then I reckon you should go ahead. Do it! Whatever it is, it's up to you."

"I have to," said Jem. She gazed with an air of tragic apology at Skye. "It's the only way I'll ever get to know!"

Me and Angel, and Mum and Dad, were all going to Speech Day. Tom could have come if he'd wanted, but like I said, he's an alien. He'd rather stay indoors and zap things on his computer than mix with real people. What with Angel being so obsessed by the opposite sex, and Tom not being quite human, I sometimes reckon I'm the only normal child that Mum and Dad have.

The hall was already filling up when we arrived. Mum and Dad went off to find seats, while me and Angel joined our year groups. I slid in next to Skye.

"Where's Jem?"

Skye nodded. "Down there. At the front."

She was sitting with the prizewinners! "Where's her mum and dad?" I twisted round to look and saw them at the end of a row. Mrs McClusky caught my eye and waved. I waved back.

"This is going to be so much fun!" I said.

It would be fun hearing Jem, it would be fun hearing Mia. It might even be fun watching all the prizewinners go up to get their prizes. It has, however, to be admitted, there are great stretches of Speech Day that are monumentally boring. I remembered from last year how the Mayor had dirged on and on, until I got all itchy with the effort of trying to sit still and not wriggle. She dirged on this year too. I don't know what she dirged about cos halfway through I zoned out (but made sure to keep a polite smile on my face in case one of the teachers was watching).

After the Mayor it was Mrs Stanhope. Nobody, I don't think, could accuse Mrs Stanhope of dirging. She has this very crisp, clear voice that forces you to pay attention. But she still went on for far too long! At least, in my opinion. Nobody wanted to hear Mrs Stanhope. *Or* the Mayor. We wanted to hear Mia!

She was sitting there on the platform, with all the dignitaries. Like a beautiful flower in a bed of weeds, I thought, poetically. I turned and whispered to Skye.

"She *could* be Jem's mum!"

Skye made a fierce hissing sound, like a goose.

"She really does look like her."

Skye went "*Sh!*" and jabbed her bony elbow into my ribs. Mrs Monteith, sitting at the end of the row, leant forward and frowned. I sank back, resigned, and rearranged my lips into their polite smile. Why *is* it that head teachers and dignitaries feel they have to go on for ever?

At last it came to an end. Mrs Stanhope was sitting down and it was Mia's turn. You could just feel everybody perking up. Unlike the Mayor, who had droned on about excellence and the importance of education in a very dreary way, the things Mia had to say were really interesting. All about when she was at the school, and how she'd always known she was going to be a performer of some kind. How she'd been accused of "always fizzing and popping". (I trod heavily on Skye's foot.) How she was regularly "put in the Book" for being late, or not paying attention, or talking in class. (We hadn't known *that*.) When she came to the bit about running away from home I dug my fingers hard into Skye's wrist, which made her jump and go "Ow!" Which made Mrs Monteith lean forward again, with an angry scowl.

"Frankie Foster," she mouthed, "behave yourself!"

I was hoping Mia might tell us why she'd run away, but she just gave a sort of rueful grin and said, "I'm afraid I'm not a very good role model. I've made some big mistakes in my time. Not exactly what you'd call a credit to the school!"

When she said this, Mrs Stanhope stretched her lips into a grimace (I think it was supposed to be a smile) and lots of people laughed.

Mia said, "No, seriously… I may have got there in the end, but please, *please*, don't anybody follow my example! It could so easily have been a total disaster. Instead of which—" She turned, brightly, to Mrs Stanhope, who grimaced again. "Here I am, a guest at Speech Day. I never would have thought it! It just shows that with enough determination, you *can* make your dreams come true."

Everyone cheered and clapped like mad. I wondered how Jem was feeling. I guessed she would be sitting there fizzing and popping, bursting with pride as she hugged her secret. The daughter of a famous celeb! I didn't care how much Skye hissed at me and jabbed me with her elbow. Mia really *could* be Jem's mum. I just didn't see how she was going to prove it. She obviously had some plan – but what?

A Year 11 girl, Kamila something or other, was called up to read her essay. It was quite interesting, all about how she came from Bosnia, but I couldn't really concentrate properly as I was too busy thinking about Jem. Suppose she *did* ask Mia, "Are you my mum?"

and Mia admitted it? What would happen? She wouldn't be able to go and live with her, cos she'd already been adopted. Maybe she'd be allowed to stay with her sometimes? Go on holiday with her. Go on *tour* with her! But what would Mr and Mrs McClusky feel? Would they be hurt? Or would they be happy for her?

While I was pondering all this, Jem came bounding on stage. She seemed to have forgotten any doubts she may have had. She was positively crackling with energy, you could almost see it shooting out of her in little darts. I turned in my seat and beamed at Mrs McClusky. Mrs McClusky beamed back. She was going to be so pleased and proud!

Jem started reading. "My beginnings are shrouded in mystery as I was adopted when I was a baby and don't remember anything about my life before. All I have been able to discover is that I was left on the steps of a churchyard—"

What? I shot a quick worried glance at Skye.

"—wrapped in a shawl. I cannot help wondering," said Jem, "what my real mum was like, and why she had to abandon me. I try not to feel bitter about it as I feel there must have been a reason. She could still, for instance, have been at school. She was probably frightened and had no one to turn to if her parents were not sympathetic."

I squirmed, uneasily, in my seat. How could Jem be so obvious? I hardly dared look in Mia's direction. Jem, meanwhile, continued regardless.

"I have this picture of her carrying me into the churchyard at dead of night, kissing me one last time – *mwah!*" She actually did it. She actually went *mwah*. Skye sat next to me, bolt upright, frozen like a block of ice.

"I imagine her praying," said Jem. "*Please—*" She closed her eyes, tilting her face heavenwards. "*Please let someone find my baby and take care of her!* I often wonder if today she still thinks of me. If she wonders where I am, and how I am getting on. I would love so much to be able to meet her and talk to her! I would love to be able to look at her and see if we are alike in any way. Whether I have her hair –" Jem turned, to beam in Mia's direction – "or her eyes. It is only natural, I think, to feel curious. Sometimes when people say to my friends, *Oh, don't you take after your mum,* I feel sad, like I am missing out. No one can ever say that to me. I don't know whether I take after my mum or not. Nobody knows! If you ask my friends what I am like, they would probably say that I am quite a fizzy, bubbly sort of person, which makes me wonder –" Jem turned again, to beam at Mia – "if my mum was also fizzy and bubbly."

My cheeks, by now, were beginning to burn. How could Jem *do* this? Did she really think

Mia was going to rush forward and throw her arms round her and announce that she was her long-lost mum? And what about Mrs McClusky? How must she be feeling?

"Before I started the search for my beginnings," continued Jem, "I discussed it with two of my friends."

Omigod! This was going from bad to worse.

"One of them, who is a very cautious person, said she thought it was best not to look, as I might not like what I found. But the other one, who is more bold, said go for it. So that is what I did. I was a bit scared in case I discovered something horrid, but once you have started it is impossible to stop. I expect people will say to me, *Was it worth it? All you have found out for sure is that you were abandoned.* But I think it is better to know than not to know. It doesn't mean that I am not grateful to my *other* mum and dad for adopting me."

I cringed, low, in my seat. I didn't dare turn to look at Mrs McClusky. I had promised her she was going to be so pleased and proud! I felt pretty dreadful.

"When you are adopted," said Jem, "you are told that you are special. And that is true, in some ways. But as this essay is supposed to be about Beginnings, I thought that I should go back as far as I can. Maybe one day I will get to meet my real mum, and then I will be able to go back even further. I really hope so."

There was a round of applause as Jem finished. I didn't applaud, and neither did Skye. We sat, stiff and silent. Other people in our class were looking around, exchanging puzzled glances. *They* knew that wasn't the essay Miss Rolfe had read out to us. Miss Rolfe herself, sitting at the side of the hall, had a face like a thundercloud. Jem was going to be in trouble.

"I told her not to do it," said Skye. "I *told* her!"

We watched as Mia handed Jem an envelope containing her book token, which was what people got for being chosen to read out their essays. We could see that Mia was saying something. Was it just congratulations or well done, or was it something else? I wished I could lipread!

When Jem had left the stage Mrs Stanhope made a few closing remarks and Speech Day came to an end. Me and Skye immediately jumped up and rushed way down to the front to grab hold of Jem. Skye said, "*Jem!*" and I squeaked, "Did she say anything?"

Before Jem could reply, her dad had appeared.

"Right." He took Jem by the arm. "Let's go. Your mum's waiting for you outside. She's very upset. Come on!"

Jem doesn't as a rule take a whole lot of notice of her dad; it's her mum who decides what's what. Mr McClusky is very quiet, he never lays down the law or even raises his voice. But that evening, at Speech Day, Jem knew better than to argue. She sent one last despairing glance at me and Skye, then obediently trailed off with her dad across the hall.

"That went well," said Skye.

She was being sarcastic. I hate when she's sarcastic!

"See you Monday." She flapped a hand.

I nodded. Skye went off to find her parents, and I looked round for Mum and Dad. I did *so* not want Mum to start going on at me! I even had this faint glimmer of hope that maybe she wouldn't have noticed anything, but of course she had.

"What was all that?" she said. "I thought you told me Jem had written lovely things about her mum and dad?"

"She changed them," I said. "*I* didn't know she was going to!"

"No?"

"No!"

"Are you telling me you had absolutely nothing to do with it?"

"Not about changing her essay!"

"What about trying to find her birth mum? Are you saying you didn't encourage her? Honestly, Frankie!" Mum shook her head. "When *will* you learn not to interfere?"

All weekend I waited for Jem to call, but she didn't. I texted her, twice. *R U OK?* and *W8ing 2 hear.* Still nothing. In the end I rang Skye to see if she had heard. She hadn't.

"D'you think we should call her?" I said.

"No." Skye sounded very definite. "She knows where we are."

"But she might think we're just not bothering!"

"I thought you said you'd texted her?"

"I have, but it's not the same."

"Look, you asked me," said Skye, "and I told you... read my lips: I DO NOT THINK WE SHOULD CALL. Wait till we see her."

It was *such* a long wait. I was out of the house really early on Monday morning, racing down the road to our meeting point. Skye arrived a few minutes later. We both scanned the horizon, anxiously waiting for Jem to appear. I thought, if she's late, it will be a bad sign. If she was bashing things with her bag, that would also be a bad sign. If she was dragging her feet, it would be an even worse sign. And then we saw her, turning the corner, coming towards us. She wasn't dragging her feet; she wasn't bashing her bag. She was *swinging* it. And skipping! Well, walking with a definite bounce.

"What happened, what happened?" I cried. "Did Mia say anything?"

"Nope!" Jem shook her head.

"She didn't admit to being your mum?"

"Nope!"

Me and Skye exchanged puzzled glances.

"She didn't admit it," said Jem, "cos she's not!"

Not? Then why was Jem so happy?

"I had this long talk with Mum… she's told me everything."

"*So?*" I jigged, impatiently. "If it wasn't Mia, who was it?"

"Nobody knows. It's a total mystery!"

Jem's face was bright pink with triumph, though I couldn't think what she had to be triumphant about. It all sounded a bit of a let down, if you asked me.

Skye looked at her, sternly. "You mean nobody knows *anything*?"

"Not very much. Just that I was abandoned."

Well, that was something. At least we'd been right about *that*.

"Just not in the churchyard," said Jem.

"So where?"

"In the hospital!"

There was a pause. Then Skye said, "In the *hospital*?"

Jem beamed, and nodded.

"What were you doing in the hospital?"

"Being born!"

"In *hospital*?"

"Yes. But only just! See, my mum – my birth mum, that is – she got there just in time. Another minute, it'd have been too late… I'd have come whooshing out in the car park! Cool, or what?" said Jem.

We gazed at her, solemnly.

"So what happened?" I said. "You got born and she abandoned you?"

"She ran off," said Jem. "Just, like, totally disappeared."

"But hang on," said Skye, "surely they'd have got her name and address? They always get people's names and addresses!"

Jem's eyes sparkled, like she was about to

let us into a big secret.

"They did," she said, "but they were *false*." Jem paused, dramatically, to let it sink in. "She made them up! When they tried to trace her they found the address didn't even exist. Neither did she! Not under the name she'd given them."

There was another pause, longer this time, while me and Skye thought about it.

"So is that all your mum knows?" I said.

"It's all anybody knows."

Not just a bit of a let down. A *total* let down. Although, on the other hand… "It still *could* have been Mia!"

"No." Jem shook her head. "She was Irish. Oh, and she had red hair and freckles, so I obviously don't take after her. Mum thinks maybe my dad might have been Italian, or something. But probably," said Jem, "I'll never know." She sighed, though she didn't sound too upset. "Mum says she'd have told me earlier if I'd asked… she wasn't deliberately keeping it from me."

"I did *say*," said Skye.

"I know, but I couldn't have asked her! You know I couldn't. I was too cross with her."

She plainly wasn't cross any more, so that was one good thing. But all that hard work! All for nothing.

"Well, at least now you know," said Skye.

I felt like saying, know what? But I didn't, cos I wouldn't have wanted to upset Jem. She was just so happy now that she and her mum were friends again, she didn't seem to mind about Mia.

"I s'pose there isn't anything much more you can do," I said.

"Well, I could," said Jem. "Mum says if I wanted I could write a letter and send it to the social services people, then if my birth mum ever gets in touch they could give it to her and she'd know where to find me."

I brightened up. "That's a good idea! Why don't we do that? Me and Skye could help. We could do it this weekend, round your place!"

"I dunno." Jem scrunched her face up. "Not sure I want to."

"But you've got to! You can't just give up."

"Maybe one day... when I'm older. I don't feel like it right now cos it really hurt Mum, me saying all those things. I don't want her to think I don't love her! I do love her. *Lots*. I know she won't let me be a model, and Liliana's got this TV commercial that will probably make her famous, but I don't care any more! I'm happy just being with Mum and Dad... my *real* mum and dad. I don't want anyone else."

Jem swished her bag, as we walked through the school gates.

"Well, I suppose, as it happens," said Skye, "things actually worked out OK. *In the end.*"

I had to agree. We might not have solved the mystery, but Jem and her mum were friends again, and that was what mattered. And in some ways, as I had to keep reminding myself, it was all down to me. After all, I was the one that had discovered the bit about Mia in the local paper. I was the one that had set it all off. If it hadn't been for me, Jem and her mum might still not be talking!

There was just one tiny thing that kept niggling at me.

"If it wasn't you that was left in the churchyard," I said, as we made our way home at the end of school, "then who was it?"

"Ah. *Well.* Yes!" Jem gave a snort, which turned into a giggle. She seemed a bit embarrassed. "It wasn't really anyone."

"You mean, it was all just made up?"

"N-no. Not exactly."

Definitely embarrassed.

"You might as well tell us," said Skye.

"Yes. Well." Jem did a little hop off the kerb and back again. "The thing is... that wasn't why Mum kept the cutting! I showed it to her, and she laughed. She told me to look at what was on the other side."

We waited.

"You know her chocolate cake?" said Jem.

You'd better believe it! We are all gluttons for Mrs McClusky's chocolate cake. It's gooey, and sticky, and totally *yum*.

"Well, that's what was on the back of it," said Jem. "My auntie sent it to her. Ages ago! For the recipe, you know? But Mum doesn't need the recipe any more, she says she could do it blindfolded she knows it off by heart, so it got stuffed in a drawer and forgotten about. She says she never even read the bit about the baby being left."

"I see." Skye nodded, gravely. "So when we went on our pilgrimage, it was all just, like, make-believe?"

Jem hung her head.

"Doesn't matter," I said. "It was fun! And the

article did say St Peter's. Not like it was St Oesophagus, or something. I mean, there's loads of St Peter's! They're all over the place."

"I know." Jem gave another little hop, not embarrassed, this time. "Mum says it's a mistake anyone could have made. Oh, and she says if you'd both like to come to tea on Friday she'll make an extra-special cake with three layers of icing!"

Things had *definitely* worked out. And all down to me!

I said goodbye to the others and whizzed on my way, impatient to get home and give Mum the good news. The minute I opened the front door Rags came bounding downstairs, all big and goofy, with this great doggy grin on his face. He flung his hairy arms round me and we collapsed in a heap on the floor, with me squeaking and Rags making the silly little yelping noises that he does when he's excited.

"What's going on?" The door of the front

room had opened and Mum had appeared. "Oh, it's you! I thought a herd of cattle was stampeding down the stairs. Frankie, come and see Emilia in her dewdrop dress."

I pulled a face. Did I have to?

"Come!" Mum held the door open. Reluctantly, I followed her through into the front room. I was a bit nervous in case I took one look and did something unforgivable, like giggling. Not that I would giggle on purpose, but sometimes these things come rushing at you without warning.

"There," said Mum. "What do you think?"

I gazed at Emilia. She stood there, pink and proud, holding out the skirt of her dress.

"Go on, then!" Her mum nudged at her. "Give us a twirl!"

Emilia twirled, and the skirt frothed and foamed. Mum and Mrs Duffy both clapped.

"Well?" said Mum. "Don't you think she makes a lovely little dewdrop?"

It was kind of surprising, but she actually did. I mean, thirteen is *way* too old to be wearing a dewdrop dress, especially if you're a bit on the large side, but Emilia just looked so sweet and so eager that I found I was suddenly clapping too.

"I reckon she ought to win first prize," I said.

"I reckon she should," said Mum.

Emilia beamed. A big banana beam that lit up her whole face.

"Off you go then!" Mum gave me a little push towards the door. "Go and put the kettle on, I'll be with you in a few minutes. Oh, and Frankie… thank you," she whispered; and she nodded at me, and smiled, like for once I had done something good.

I bundled off down the hall with Rags, walloping at him playfully with my school bag. I love it when I have Mum's approval! It doesn't happen all that often.

Angel was in the kitchen, texting someone,

her thumbs flying about all over the place. She prides herself on being this champion texter. When me and Rags came bursting in she shouted, "Oh, God!" at the top of her voice and went rushing out, still texting. She is completely mad.

She is also very messy; the whole table was covered in her stuff. Books, and pens, and sticks of make-up. A hairbrush (with *hair* in it). Bits of used tissue. Her purse, her keys, a packet of chewing gum, with a lump of chewed gum stuck on to it. Everything just rolling about. Quite disgusting, really. I mean the gum, and the hair. Yuck! I knew what had happened. Her phone had started ringing, and in her eagerness to get to it she'd simply upended her bag and tipped out the contents on the kitchen table. Well, they could stay there! Wasn't my job to tidy up after her.

I put the kettle on and went into the garden with Rags, where we played with his ball for a while until it suddenly occurred to me that the clump of dead sticks he was trampling on might not be dead sticks at all, they might be some sort of plant. In which case, Mum would not be happy.

I decided to go back in and do something noble to make up for it. Just in case. I would clear away Angel's mess and I would lay the table! Nicely, the way Mum likes it. Sometimes, if she's been working late, we just make a little bit of space at one end, with everything all scrunched up. When we do that Mum says things like, "Oh, your nan would despair!" or "Whatever happened to proper family meals?" She would be pleased if she came out to find knives and forks and plates all properly laid out, and I wouldn't feel so guilty about the plant. If it was a plant.

I picked up Angel's bag and started scooping stuff into it. I chucked the tissues into the bin but I left the lump of chewing gum. I wasn't touching *that*, thank you very much. The book was lying open, so I thought maybe she'd been doing her homework, but then I saw that it was called *Fangs of Love* and had a black cover with bright red blood dripping down from the title. Cool! I wondered if she'd let me borrow it when she was done. I like books with black covers, especially if they have blood on them.

I thought I'd better mark the place as she would only get mean if I didn't, so I laid the book, very carefully, face down and still open, on top of the dresser. I didn't even dog-ear the page; I didn't want to give her anything to moan about.

Mum came in just as the kettle was boiling.

"Look!" I said. "I laid the table for you."

"Lovely," said Mum. "That makes me very happy."

"I thought you'd like it," I said. "Oh, and I wanted to tell you… you know you said about me interfering? With Jem? Looking for her birth mum? Well, she and her mum have made it up. They're friends again. And it's all down to me!"

"Really," said Mum.

"Yes, cos if I hadn't pushed her – not that I did! I didn't *push*. I just had the idea. And you said I shouldn't have, but if I hadn't she and her mum might still not be talking. And now they are! So it's all worked out. So that's good, isn't it?"

"It is," said Mum. "I'm glad to hear it. Go and tell your brother and sister that tea's ready."

That was all she had to say? I'd thought she might at least have apologised, or something. Accusing me of interfering!

Mum said, "Frankie?"

"Yeah, OK." I went into the hall and yelled, *"AN-GEL! TOM! TEA'S READY!"*

"Thank you," said Mum. "Remind me to put some ear plugs in next time."

What did she think? I was going to go all the way upstairs?

Tom came into the kitchen just as Dad arrived back from work. Mum said, "There, now, isn't that nice? All of us sitting down together, for once."

"Except Angel," I said. "D'you want me to call her again?"

"Yeah, try shouting a bit louder," said Tom. "Put a bit of effort into it." He sniggered. "Couldn't hardly hear you before."

Excuse me? Mr Kaye, who takes us for drama, says I have this really POWERFUL voice. I don't go all high and shrill like Angel; anyone would have to be deaf, not to hear me. But I went back out to the hall and bellowed obediently up the stairs: "ANGEL-MUM-WANTS-US-ALL-TO-SIT-DOWN-TOGETHER!"

Dad had his hands over his ears. "That's grievous bodily harm, that is," he said.

"Tom said I didn't shout loud enough!"

Tom sniggered again.

"I think you'll find he was being funny," said Mum. "Still, at least she'll have heard you this time… along with half the neighbourhood."

Seconds later, Angel's footsteps came clunking down the stairs.

"You didn't have to *shout*," she said. "I'm not *deaf*." And then she looked at the table, laid for tea, and shrieked, "*What have you done with my stuff?*"

Dad's hands flew back to his ears. I pointed silently at the dresser.

"What about my book mark? Where's my bookmark?"

"It's all right," I said. "I've saved your place."

"BUT WHERE'S THE BOOKMARK?"

Dad groaned.

I said, "There wasn't any bookmark."

I might as well not have bothered: Angel just went on shrieking.

"Where is it? What have you done with it?"

She tipped up her bag, scattered the contents and began madly scrabbling through. "Where has it gone? My autograph from Robbie!"

Dad said, "Who's Robbie, when he's at home?"

"He's this boy at my school," said Tom. "He's in Year 11 and he's got this band called Death's Head and all the girls go stupid about him."

"He signed my hankie," wailed Angel.

"If you mean that bit of old tissue," I said, "I put it in the bin."

"*In the bin?*" Angel's voice rose to a bat squeak. Dad winced. "You put Robbie's autograph *in the bin*?"

"I didn't know it was an autograph!" Who goes round collecting autographs on paper hankies? Not to mention using them as bookmarks. "It just looked like a bit of used tissue to me."

"GOD!" Angel hurled herself at the bin and threw back the lid. "Ugh! Yuck!" She pulled out a sodden tissue. "This was my most treasured possession and you've gone and ruined it!"

"Oh, now, be fair," said Mum, "she didn't mean to. She was only trying to help! She was laying the table for me."

"She didn't have to go and throw my autograph in the bin! Why can't she just leave my things alone? I'll never forgive you for this," panted Angel. "Never, as long as I live! My autograph from Robbie!"

"I'm sure Tom could get you another," said Mum.

Tom looked startled.

"Or maybe we could dry it out. Let me have it."

Resentfully, Angel said, "It's got *muck* on it."

"It's only a bit damp, don't panic. We'll put it on some kitchen roll and it'll dry out just fine."

"If it's that important," I said, "you should have got it laminated."

Angel turned on me, furiously. "You can't laminate a paper tissue!"

"Well, or you could have stuck it in an autograph book, or something. That's what I'd have done."

"I'm not interested in what you'd have done! You've already *done* it, as far as I'm concerned."

Mum laughed. "For goodness' sake! Stop being so melodramatic."

"But it's my autograph from Robbie!"

"I'm sorry," I said. "*I* didn't know."

Angel made a sound like, "Humph!"

"Sit down and eat your tea," said Mum.

"I don't want any tea!" Angel had her mobile out, and was frantically texting again. "I'm going back upstairs!"

The door slammed behind her.

"Well, I never," said Dad. "Poor old Frankie!" He pulled a sympathetic face. "Can't do anything right, can you?"

Mum put her arm round me. "Don't worry,

beanie, it's not the end of the world." *Beanie*. That was my pet name when I was little. "You know what your sister's like… a bit of a drama queen."

I was really grateful that for once both Mum and Dad were on my side. Quite an unusual state of affairs! But as Mum had said, I was only trying to help. It's all I ever do; I don't set out on purpose to upset people. Not even Angel. I don't *like* upsetting her.

"She'll get over it," said Mum.

In the meantime, I reminded myself that it was entirely thanks to me that Jem was happy again. I might have chucked my sister's most treasured possession in the waste bin, but at least I had helped one of my two best friends make it up with her mum. That had to be worth something!

"Funny, funky, feisty - and fantastic reads!" JACQUELINE WILSON

FRANKIE FOSTER

Pick 'n' Mix

Here to Help!

Jean Ure

… Out in July!

Can't wait until then? Turn over for a

sneak preview…

All I'm saying is, I didn't set out to cut a hole. It wasn't like I woke up in the morning and thought, "Today I shall cut a hole in my carpet." It just seemed like a good idea at the time, as things so often do. Then afterwards you wonder why, only by then it's too late. This is something that happens to me rather a lot. I am quite unfortunate in that way.

What I was doing, in actual fact, wasn't thinking about cutting holes so much as trying to find a way of fitting my corner cabinet into a corner. Gran had given me the cabinet when she moved out of her house into a flat. It's really cute! Very small and painted white, with pink and blue flowers all running round the edge, and tiny glass-panelled doors. Gran used to keep china ornaments in there. Shepherdesses and milkmaids and old-fashioned ladies selling balloons. I keep my collection of shells and fossils and interesting stones with holes in them. Gran knew I'd always loved her corner cabinet. I was so excited when she gave it to me! But the thing is, it is a *corner* cabinet. That is why it is shaped like a triangle. It has to stand in a *corner*.

I've only got two corners in my bedroom. This is because it's the smallest room in the house, tucked away under the roof, and is shaped like a wedge of cheese. The big front bedroom is Mum and Dad's; the one at the back is Angel's; the little one over the garage is Tom's; and the one the size of a broom cupboard belongs to me. Mum says that when

Angel goes to uni, Tom can have her room and I can have his. And when *Tom* goes to uni, I can take over. But since Angel is only fifteen, it seems to me I'm going to be stuck in my broom cupboard for years to come.

I don't really mind; I quite like my little bedroom. It's cosy, like a nest. And I love the way the roof slopes down, and the way the window is at floor level. The only problem is, is the lack of corners! My bed is in one, and my wardrobe in the other. I'd tried fitting Gran's cabinet into the angle between the roof and the floor, but it was just the *tiniest* little bit too tall. If I could only slice a couple of centimetres off the bottom of it …

That was when it came to me. If I couldn't slice anything off Gran's cabinet, how about cutting a hole in the carpet? It just seemed like the obvious solution! What Dad calls *lateral thinking*. I reckoned he would be quite pleased with me. He is always telling us to "think outside the box" and "use your imagination." That was exactly what I was doing!